FEDERAL OFFENSE

FEDERAL OFFENSE

BY
VENEDA (SAMMI) REED

COVER ILLUSTRATED BY
JAMES E. HATHAWAY

COPYRIGHT © 2010 BY VENEDA (SAMMI) REED.

LIBRARY OF CONGRESS CONTROL NUMBER:		2010911614
ISBN:	HARDCOVER	978-1-4535-5430-2
	SOFTCOVER	978-1-4535-5429-6
	EBOOK	978-1-4535-5431-9

All rights reserved. No part of this book may be reproduced or transmitted in any form or by any means, electronic or mechanical, including photocopying, recording, or by any information storage and retrieval system, without permission in writing from the copyright owner.

This is a work of fiction. Names, characters, places and incidents either are the product of the author's imagination or are used fictitiously, and any resemblance to any actual persons, living or dead, events, or locales is entirely coincidental.

This book was printed in the United States of America.

To order additional copies of this book, contact:
Xlibris Corporation
1-888-795-4274
www.Xlibris.com
Orders@Xlibris.com

DEDICATION

To Debby who urged me on day to day
and for the torture of waiting for the next chapter.

Chapter One

The muddy road made it hard to maneuver the rusty old Country Squire station wagon, as the distraught woman raced along the ruts and through the puddles. Because of the speed she was trying to maintain, the car was swerving and lurching from side to side while she struggled to keep it under control. With all of the bouncing and swerving, her headlights seemed to be dancing all around, which made it even harder to tell where she was going most of the time. Her eyes kept darting back and forth between the road and the rear view mirror as she thought to herself. *I know that car was following me. I'm going to get caught. I know I am. Oh god, I can't let that happen. I knew I should have gotten a sports car or something like that. I've got to get back onto a main highway, where I can make better time. But first I have to make sure that I've lost whoever was following me.* She checked the rear view mirror again and again. She saw no sign of headlights, but she wasn't going to take any chances. She needed to keep going.

Just then a petite blonde haired girl that was crouched down on the floorboard of the passenger's side of the vehicle cries out, "What's wrong? Why can't I get up?" The little girl's big blue eyes would have shown the great fear in them, if it hadn't have been so dark, but the woman was in such a state of panic and too preoccupied with making her get-away to notice, even if she could have seen them.

The woman snapped back at the child, out of fear more than anger. "Don't you move. You stay down there." She checked her rear view mirror one more time, still no sign of a pursuing vehicle.

"I'm scared," the tiny voice replied from the floorboard.

"Not now, can't you see I'm busy," The woman snapped at the child once again. Just then the car hit a patch of gravel and the woman quickly compensated one more time. The car's rear end swerved from side to side then dug in as the woman stepped down harder on the accelerator. She felt her body press back against the seat as the car responded. She did have to admit that for a rusty old wagon this car did have power. Maybe she was right to choose it after all.

The little girl curled up on the floorboard with her arms wrapped firmly around her folded legs and held her breath. She pinched her eye closed as tightly as possible, wishing she could make this terrible thing that was happening just go away.

Up ahead the woman spotted a crossroad sign. "Alright maybe we've found pavement. Now we can make better time." She looked down at her speedometer and smiled, *seventy miles an hour*. If she could get on a paved road now she could make even better time. She checked her rear view mirror. Still no lights were behind her. *Now, if I can avoid the cops I can be out of this state and into the next one by daylight.* She felt safer traveling at night. It made them less noticeable and the last thing she needed was to be noticed.

She spotted the intersection up ahead and started to feel a sense of relief. This feeling was short lived though as she noticed the flashing lights from a police car. *Oh no, not now. I can't get caught, now, after all of this time. That cop must have been on a side road. Why wasn't I more careful? I should have been checking there too. How dumb can I be? I can't let him catch us. I've got to get away.* She punched the gas once more and darted toward the paved road as she started to yank the wheel to the right. The car responded with a lurch when it hit the protrusion where the pavement met the gravel. As though in slow motion, the car catapulted to the opposite side of the road, slamming into a tree.

The police car pulled up along side of the contorted old wagon, while the neatly pressed officer frantically spoke into his mike, "Peggy, send the fire rescue unit and the chief out to the intersection of Grand and Oak. There's been an accident." Then he bailed out of his cruiser and ran to the wagon. Approaching the driver's side, he noticed the woman in her mid twenties was bleeding from her head and wasn't moving. He placed his fingers to the left side of the woman's neck. He felt a very faint pulse. "Hold on lady help is on the way." He ran back to the patrol car and once again picked up the mike and spoke into it. "Peggy you'd better have air rescue be ready to fly. This looks bad. Tell the rescue unit that we have a woman in her mid to late twenties pinned in her car. There is trauma to the head and the steering wheel is pushed into her chest. I have a faint pulse at the moment."

He grabbed a blanket from the trunk of the cruiser and ran back to the woman. He did his best to cover her, then kept trying to give her words of encouragement, to let her know that she wasn't alone, until the medics arrived.

The woman seemed to be almost anorexic with blonde hair. She had been on the road for a while by the looks of things. Other than being under weight she was dressed in expensive clothing and had obviously been well kept in the past, but had seen some hard road recently. The old rusty wagon didn't seem to be the sort of car this woman should be driving. A much more expensive vehicle would have suited this woman more, the Officer thought.

The woman made no movement, but moaned a little. Other than that, she showed little signs of being coherent. The Officer looked over the situation as he waited for help. The car was steaming from the rupture in the radiator and the front end was folded around the tree. The rest was pushed back onto the woman. This didn't look good. He kept trying to stimulate the woman enough to keep her awake until the medics arrived. "Come on Lady, open your eyes. Help is coming. You have to try hard to stay awake."

FEDERAL OFFENSE

The lady mumbled again. It sounded as though she was saying, "pen."

"Pen," the officer asked. "Why do you want a pen?"

The lady just kept on mumbling then fell silent just as the medics arrived.

The young officer stood back to give the medics room to work as he wondered to himself if there wasn't more he could have done. He felt himself shiver then the warm hand of the Chief was placed on his shoulder.

The chief's voice was calm, as he said, "Step over here son and tell me what happened. The medics will take it from here."

The rescue unit had to use the Jaws of Life and worked frantically to treat the woman as much as possible, before removing her from the wreck. They loaded her into the helicopter and it flew off to the hospital. The auto-wrecking yard sent out a flatbed truck to haul off what was left of the car. The truck backed up to prepare to hook onto the car with its winch. The young officer was explaining to the Chief of police what had happened as they searched though the wreckage to find any paperwork on the car and identification for the woman.

Just then the young officer noticed something and gasped. A tiny little hand reached out from under the dash, where it had been pulled back enough to free the woman. The officer through his hands up in the air and yelled. "Everybody stop. Then turned back toward the car and said out of horror, "Oh my god."

9

Chapter Two

My day started out like most any other day in the small town of Westfield. After beating on the top of my alarm clock until it stopped beeping, I sat on the edge of my couch for quite some time, rubbing my eyes and trying to clear the cobwebs from my brain. I was having the usual mental argument with myself to get moving. Finally I forced myself to stand up and let out my usual moan as my stiff joints rebelled. I straightened my oversized T-shirt that I use as a nightgown, then stumbled to the dresser, which was next to the bathroom door. I pulled out a clean T-shirt, underclothes, socks and a pair of jeans, then staggered into the bathroom. My studio was very small. It consisted or a kitchenette, a couch, dresser, desk, file cabinet, bookcase and coffee table, which accounted for all of the wall space. But it was big enough for me. Of course when my son, Jesse, came by on break from College, which he would be doing the next day, he always brought his camping cot. That made things rather tight, but it was cozy. We didn't need that much room, because when Jesse was home, we spent little time at the studio. We always dreamed up something to do with the little time we had together. Of course this was summer break, so we would have more time than usual to play.

I stood in the shower for quite some time letting the water wash over me. I was still arguing with myself about going into the office.

As I got dressed and looked in the mirror at the reflection looking back at me, I noticed my bloodshot eyes and black hair with a trim of gray down the sides, which I kept fairly short. I wasn't the type to have to spend a lot of time getting ready while half asleep in the morning. The less muss and fuss the better. It seemed to me as though I had even more wrinkles than the day before. "Ricky," I admitted out loud to myself, "I do believe you are getting too old for this." I told myself this most every morning, but I also knew I'd charge at another day and give it all I had to give, once I had my morning coffee of course.

I looked back on my younger years. Being raised on a farm and working like a mule, when I was a kid, by the time I reached my twenties I was in pretty good physical shape. Granted I had already formed an ulcer from worrying and several stiff joints from broken bones, but over all I was strong, back then. I didn't let anything stop me. Now here I am in my forties and there are mornings that I feel like I'm eighty and all I want to do is crawl back into the bed and sleep the day away. I can't of course, because that doesn't earn a paycheck or pay the bills. Somehow life isn't fair. Once you know what you want to do with your life your too old and worn out to do it.

After muttering to myself for a few minutes, I ran a brush through my hair, swished the toothbrush around in my mouth and headed out the door of my messy studio apartment, with papers scattered everywhere, making a mental note to pick up a bit before Jesse got home. I headed down the street to the Hitching Post for breakfast.

The Hitching Post was a restaurant in town that my friend Becky worked at and had done so since before my family moved here. I had spent almost every morning for the last eight years having coffee there with Becky, before heading off to work. This was my usual morning routine. Of course this was suppose to be my day off, but I was just going into the office for a while to put some finishing touches on some paperwork. I hoped to get back to the studio and straighten up. I didn't want anything hanging over my head, with Jesse coming home for the summer.

Mrs. Wiggins' puppy ran up to me for it's morning scratch behind the ear then plodded back to the step and waited for Mrs. Wiggins to set out the morning feast.

Mrs. Wiggins was an Elderly widow that had a small cottage next door to my studio. Sometimes in the evening I would sit outside with her and listen to her stories about her life and times. She was a sweet lady, but got lonely since her husband past away. I've always enjoyed listening to stories of a time long since gone.

I chuckled at the puppy, as he waited anxiously for Mrs. Wiggins to appear at the door. Even though he was sitting, his front paws were doing a little dance of their own. His tail was wagging some hard that it made the rest of his body wiggle. "You stay there, Herbie," I said to the wiggling pup. "I'm sure your food is on its way." I chuckled again, shook my head and continued on down the street.

As I walked on, Ralph, a retired race car driver that started his own taxi service of one car, drove by and waved. He was making his usual morning run to the small commuter airport in the next town. Ralph's old taxi didn't look like much on the outside, but everybody in town knew that the racing wasn't out of Ralph's blood. The engine was built and fine-tuned for maximum speed and performance. As usual he hoped there would be someone, at the Airport, in need of his services. I returned a wave and a smile as I continued on my way to the Hitching Post. It was the same thing every morning.

When I walked in the front door of the Hitching Post, I could smell the coffee brewing and bacon frying on the grill. As I walked up to the counter and planted myself on the stool, my friend Becky placed a cup of coffee in front of me. "Maybe I should leave you the whole pot, Ricky. It looks like you could use it." Becky gave a quick joking smile, then asked, "Another long night at the courthouse?"

"Ya," I replied, "Same old crap, just a different day. I'm glad that case is over with." I shook my head. "You know when I got my private investigator's license I thought it was going to be a whole lot more exciting than tracking down papers for a small time lawyer and stroking people's egos, but what the heck it's a living." I took a couple of swallows of my coffee and Becky tipped up the pot, to top off my cup.

VENEDA (SAMMI) REED

The Hitching Post was nearly empty this time of morning and I liked that, because I could bend Becky's ear for a while before the breakfast rush started and she'd stand over me with the coffee pot until the fog in my head started to clear.

Becky was in her late forties, which made her and I around the same age. She was better at listening than any bartender I had ever known and believe me in my younger years I was on the first name bases with a lot of bartenders. Becky stood about five seven. She was stocky in build and had black wavy hair that hung just below her shoulders. She had a dry sense of humor and when people first met her they weren't sure how to take her. Once they did get to know her, they couldn't help but like her. Becky was more up front and bluntly honest then anyone I had ever met. I guessed that's what I liked about her the most. There was no guessing where you stood with Becky.

I sipped more of my coffee as Becky remarked, "Oh come on Ricky, it's better than killing yourself on that construction crew, like you were doing all the time your kids were growing up and it's nowhere near as hard on your body." Becky topped off my cup again.

"Ya, I know," I answered, "I'm just tired I guess." Then I smiled at her and said, "maybe I just haven't found what I really want to do with my life when I grow up."

Becky released one of her boisterous laughs as she replied, "Have any of us? Besides, who wants to grow up?"

I shock my head and responded. "You got a point there."

Just then old Ned, the chief of police spoke up. I must have still been half-asleep when I walked into the Hitching Post that morning, because until that moment I hadn't even noticed him sitting at the other end of the counter.

The Hitching Post had a fairly large dining room, with two sets of booths that ran down the center and a short partition between them. This gave the place a look of being smaller than it really was. My favorite spot was at the half-round counter, in front of the kitchen. It was like a big conversation center at times, once the morning people started filtering in. It was still early though, so Becky, Ned and I were the only ones there except for Jake, the owner and head cook.

Jake was in the kitchen making sure that everything was just right for the morning rush. Jake was a good cook and attracted most of the business in our town and the surrounding towns as well.

Ned, the Chief of Police, had to be in his late fifties or early sixties. He was about five ten with graying brown hair. His belly hung over his belt buckle considerably. We always teased him about his belly and told him it was from years of eating to many doughnuts. Ned always laughed and agreed, then added, "That and Jake's cooking." He was a sweet man and had a great love for this town and we the same for him. With that belly of his, Ned did make a good Santa Claus for St. Christopher's children's ward every year. He didn't need much stuffing and he was great with the kids.

He got up and moved to the stool next to me and said, "Well Ricky, if you're bored, I've got something for you to look into that might just peak your interest."

FEDERAL OFFENSE

"What have you got in mind Ned," I asked. I couldn't imagine anything happening at the Westfield police station much more interesting than what was happening in my office, which was very little.

I was just finishing up a border dispute case. Old man Picket wanted to put up a new fence line and old man Bartlett claimed that Picket was fencing off his property. My job was to look up the old deeds and try to figure them out for the surveyor. Picket's great grandfather laid out the boundary line between the two pieces of land back in the 1800's. According to his papers the boundary ran between the rock pile he had cleared from the north field and the old pine tree he had put the kid's tree house in.

Needless to say trying to find that boundary line was a real feat. The tree was long dead or removed and there were more rock piles than pasture out there. After months of admiring livestock and stroking egos I managed to get them to agree on the boundary lines and the surveyor quickly marked it off and recorded it, before they had a chance to change their minds.

I liked the quiet life in Westfield most of the time. That's why I moved here, but I had to admit at times it could use a little shaking up and I wasn't sure that anything that came out of Ned's office was going to shake things up in my life. How wrong I was! The events to follow changed my life forever and sent shock waves through the lives of everyone that was close to me.

Chapter Three

"Well," Ned started to tell me about the case that he wanted me to look into. "We had an accident on the outskirts of town lastnight. A car was speeding and hit a tree. The lady that was driving never made it to the hospital. She was in bad shape when she left the scene and was declared DOA at the hospital."

"That's too bad, Ned, but what can I do about that," I responded, trying to urge him to get to the point.

"There was also a little girl in the car. She was curled up on the floorboard when the rescue team pried the dash back. She's in the hospital at Saint Christopher's," Ned continued, "There was no I.D. on either the woman or the child or in the car."

"That's strange," I said. He was beginning to catch my interest now. "No identification at all you say?"

Ned nodded his head in answer to my question. "Ricky, I can't go traipsing all over the country trying to find this little girl's family. I have a job here. It's not exciting, but it's my responsibility."

"So you want me to try to find them?"

"At least see the girl and see what you think," Ned requested.

"Well . . . I have to run by the office a clear up a little paper work first, but give me what you've got on her and I'll look into it. It might be interesting at that."

Ned explained, "The little girl looks to be five or six years old. She's in room 345 in St. Christopher's children's ward. She hasn't said a word to anyone. I think she's scared of all the strangers huddling around her. You've had kids, maybe you'll be able to get something out of her."

"Ya, I had kids," I replied, "But I was lucky. My kids were different than most. They raised me." I chuckled. It was partly true. I believe that the kids and I raised each other.

My husband and I had separated when the kids were pretty young, so from that time on, at times it seemed as though it was my two kids and I against the world. We worked together to make a home. We laughed together and cried together and everyday was a struggle just to get by, but we made it and I believe my children are what held me together over the years.

I couldn't afford to crumble under the pressure, because they needed me. I couldn't afford to be out of work because my income was all we had, so I worked and they held the home together. Due to these events in our lives my children decided at a young age to set their goals high, so they wouldn't end up in my shoes some day. I loved them more than life itself, but that was just *my* kids.

"Will you try?" Ned looked desperate.

"Oh, what the heck, I've got nothing else, that important, to do right now." I did have to admit that I was intrigued. I can't say that I was crazy about kids, because most of them seemed spoiled rotten to me, but I did have a great relationship with my own. Maybe it was possible I might hit it off with this one. After all, Ned said this kid was all alone and that did make me feel sorry for her. "Did you run a trace on the car," I asked.

"I'm doing that right now. I hope to have an answer soon. But I'm worried about the kid." Ned was an old softy at heart.

"Okay Ned, I'll go see her as soon as I get done at the office." I finished my coffee and started to pull out my wallet.

Becky reached across the counter and held me down on my stool. "Not before you eat. I know you Ricky. Once you get wrapped up in something you forget to eat and run yourself down. Now sit." She ordered breakfast for me and watched over me until I ate it all.

When I finished I looked up at her and said, "Can I go now mommy," in a joking manner.

She chuckled and said, "That's better."

I paid my tab, tipped Becky and got up from the counter.

As I turned to leave. Becky called after me. "Ricky you have a tendency to wear your heart on your sleeve. Protect it."

"I'm getting tougher every day," I replied.

"Ya, Right," She returned in a tone that said she didn't believe a word of it. Becky was right, but I'd never admit it. Becky knew me better than most people. I guess that you get to know someone pretty well after pouring coffee for her every morning for eight years.

When my kids were growing up I had convinced most of the town of Westfield that I was tough as nails and would beat the tar out of anyone that hurt my kids. My kids always thought it was funny, but they also used me as an excuse for not getting into trouble with the other kids. All they would have to say is, "You know my Mom," and the other kids would suddenly understand. Becky, however, always saw through my act, but I saw through her act too. She also acted a little rough around the edges, but down deep inside she was even softer than either Ned or me. Becky had a heart of gold and would give you the shirt off her back. If you were hurting she was hurting too, if she took a liking to you, because once that happened you became family. If she didn't like you or didn't trust you, she'd let you know that too, in no uncertain terms.

As I left the Hitching Post, I started mulling over in my mind, what little information Ned had given me. Had that woman kidnapped the kid or was the kid really hers? Why was there no identification on them or in the car somewhere? The woman had to be running from something, but what? Maybe I could sink my teeth into this case after all. I only hoped that I was qualified enough to get the answers without messing everything up.

I practically ran to the office. I did a quick redraft on my report, set it on the bosses desk, along with a note reminding him I was taking some time off to be with Jesse. I locked up the office and headed to the hospital.

When I first moved to Westfield I was surprised to see that such a small town had a hospital, such as St Christopher's. I was told that Thaddeus Jenkins, a small town doctor, who needed some place to bring his more serious cases to monitor their treatments, started it. Little by little additions where made, as people from the surrounding towns chose Doc. Jenkins' personalized care. Soon Doctors from surrounding areas started a rotation system between their own hospitals and Doc Jenkins' rapidly growing practice. Today St. Christopher's is a beautiful big hospital in the middle of a small town. People still file in from surrounding towns for the personalized care they feel they receive here.

As I walked into St Christopher's I felt a cold chill run down my spine. I hated hospitals. It wasn't just because of the cold sterile environment that made me dread them. Too many times I've lost family members and dear friends in them. To me people seemed to go in, but seldom came back out. Deep down inside I knew that wasn't true, but convincing my heart of this point was a different story. I hesitated inside the door for a moment, then shook off my feeling of dread and headed for the elevator, hit the up arrow and waited.

Just then a voice came from behind me, "Hello Ricky, Ned told me he was going to try to talk you into working on this case, but I didn't think he'd actually succeed in doing it."

I was concentrating so hard on forcing myself to get into the elevator that the voice startled me a bit. I spun around to come face to face with Kyle Jefferson, one of Ned's officers. He had gone to high school with my daughter, Annie and was fresh out of the police academy. He stood about six feet tall and was as skinny as a rail. His sandy, blonde hair was neatly trimmed and his uniform kept in perfect order. Being straight from the academy he was still wet behind the ears, but what the heck, so was I. "Why didn't you think I'd take the case," I asked, returning to reality.

Kyle grinned, "Oh I guess I never took you for someone that was that crazy about kids, say nothing about one you didn't even know. I know that you, Jesse and Annie are close, but you never seemed to be very thrilled about being around other kids."

"I'm not, but this case intrigues me," I replied.

Kyle nodded, "Ya, me too. Did the chief tell you that I was the one that found the girl?"

"No. He didn't tell me that. I'm sorry Kyle that must have been quite a shocking scene."

"I know I have to expect this kind of thing from time to time, but all I was trying to do was stop the lady for speeding. I didn't mean to spook her and I have to tell you, Rick when that little girl's hand appeared out from under that dash I almost cried. We were getting ready to load the car on to the flatbed and haul it off." He paused for a moment then continued, "Damn, what would have happened if I hadn't spotted her hand when I did." Kyle's face turned pale from the thought.

"Don't even think about that. You did find her. That's what counts," I replied. I remembered Kyle from when he was in high school. He was a smart kid; in fact he had skipped two grades, which made him younger than his classmates. He was quiet then and very sensitive to the feeling of others. He had comforted Annie a couple of times, when we first moved here and the other kids teased her, because she was the new girl.

Kyle gave a sickly smile and said, "Ya, I guess you're right."

"I know I'm right," I said with a joking grin.

Kyle let out a little chuckle as the door of the elevator opened.

As we stepped onto the elevator, we both fell silent and I knew that Kyle was running the same questions through his head as I was. Kyle led me to the little girl's room and said, "I'll leave you alone. I'll be in the cafeteria when you're done. Stop by and let me know how it went."

I nodded and said, "I will Kyle," And he started to walk away. "Kyle," I called after him and he turned to face me. "You did good you know."

He smiled and said, "Thanks Ricky." Then he stood up a little straighter and headed to the cafeteria.

I stood there a moment and watched him until he turned the corner. I had to admit that he was a good kid. Too many kids now days seemed to be heading down the path of destruction, and didn't seem to care who they took along with them. Maybe I was being cynical or maybe just getting old. I remembered adults saying something similar when I was young and I thought they were crazy at the time.

After a while I turned and walked into the little girl's room. In the hospital bed surrounded by books and teddy bears was a little wisp of a girl with light blonde hair that looked almost transparent and big blue eyes. She was staring at the ceiling with a blank look on her face. I felt a sadness sweep over me. What horrors could cause such a beautiful little child to have such a blank stare? Her little arms were lying on top of the blankets and I looked down at her tiny little fingers and imagined them reaching out from under a crumpled up dash. It gave me a shiver. I thought about Kyle and how he most have felt, witnessing this. I made a mental note to reassure him next time I saw him.

Standing over the little girl was Doctor Jenkins with a look that spooked me when he turned to focus on me. "Ricky," he said, sounding shocked. "Could I see you outside for a moment please."

I was puzzled by his request, but I nodded and stepped back out into the hallway. Dr. Jenkins patted the little girl's hand gently and followed me out the door.

Doctor Jenkins was an older man with graying hair and wire rimmed glasses. He stood about three inches shorter than me and had a bit of a hunch in his back, I guessed from all those years of bending over hospital beds. He was the head of the children's ward and was widely respected. St. Christopher's was his grandfather's dream. His great grandfather had a small practice in Westfield years ago and delivered all the children in this town in the old days and half of the livestock as well. This was back when Doctor's made house calls and was much more informal. Doctor Jenkins was much like his grandfather and great grandfather, because he believed in treating the whole patient, not just the ailment.

As the door to the room closed the good Doctor placed his hand on my shoulder and guided me away from the door, out of earshot of the room. "I see Ned *did* talk you into taking the case."

"Why does everyone seem so surprised?" I was starting to get annoyed. Then I started to wonder, was this why he asked me out into the hall. Did he think I was so dead set against kids that I shouldn't be on this case? Was he going to recommend that I not take it?

"I don't know," Jenkins replied. I know you always had a special connection to your own children, I could see that when you brought them in to see me, when they were little, but you never struck me as the type to want to deal with anyone else's children."

"That's what Kyle said too. You're right though, but mainly because of what I see out there on the streets today. I don't have the patience for it. This is different. Maybe I won't be able to get through to this kid, but I won't know until I try." Then I remarked, "she sure is a frail little thing isn't she."

"More than you know Ricky. I need to explain her case to you before you go in there," Jenkins started.

"Ned has filled me in," I answered.

"No Ricky, I mean I have to tell you what I have found out from my examination." Jenkins seemed intense.

"Okay," I said, "What do you have for me." The look on his face made me uncomfortable. I had seen this look before and it usually meant trouble.

"The injuries from the accident are superficial, but prior to that this child has been through hell," he stated.

"What kind of hell," I asked.

"This child has had several broken bones in the past, in my opinion was do to physical abuse," he replied.

I felt my body start to tense up with anger.

Jenkins started shaking as he continued. "She has also been sexually assaulted in a very brutal manner I would say over a long period of time."

Now an intense feeling of rage swept over me. I started shaking as though I was cold. I had a tendency to do that when I was angry beyond reason or had any intense feelings. "Are you saying that this tiny little thing has been raped?"

I could see the tears forming in his eyes as he nodded. "There is going to have to be some reconstructive surgery done and she'll never be able to have children of her own some day. There's too much damage." Doctor Jenkins was a professional, so to see him tear up in that manner explained the severity of the situation.

I sunk to the chair that was behind me in the hallway. "Oh my god!" I felt sick to my stomach and my mind started reeling with so many thoughts that I felt dizzy. How was I to handle this situation? Could I do the wrong thing for this child? Being abused as I child myself, I remembered when someone did believe me and tried to help, matters usually got worse. I didn't want to do that to this little girl. Maybe I didn't want to find her family. In cases like this the possibilities of a family member being responsible was quite high. What if the family didn't know? How would I tell them if I did find them?

I sat there and thought about the whole situation for quite a while, as well as fighting off the sudden flood of memories that had been deeply buried in the back of my mind. Finally I let out a deep shaky sigh and got to my feet. "Well, I've got to try to get through to her. We'll never know the whole story if I don't. I promise not to push her." I was battling with my emotions while trying to put forth an air of confidence.

"I'd appreciate that Ricky," Jenkins replied as he studied my face. I had the feeling he was seeing right through my act and that made me uneasy. I was supposed to be a professional, not shaken up like this. Of course he had no doubt seen many more of these cases and he still looked a bit shaken, so I guessed I wasn't doing so badly after all.

Chapter Four

After my talk with Doctor Jenkins I braced myself for the worst and walked back into the little girl's hospital room and looked at the helpless child lying on the big bed in this strange place. She had to wonder if all of her life was meant to be the way she had lived so far. I remembered those same feelings. I remembered wandering if I was ever going to live long enough to have a happy life and live like other people I knew in the world. Were they really happy or were they just better at hiding it than I was? It was a horrible feeling and I wondered if this tiny child felt that same way.

I walked over to the bed, released a sigh and started talking. "Well young lady, you have quite a selection of books here. Do you mind if I read them to you? I like reading to kids. My daughter and I spent many hours together reading books." Then I shrugged my shoulders a bit and said, "My son on the other hand could never sit still long enough to listen." I chuckled as I thought back. "He was a holly terror, but you should see him now. He's a pretty special young man," I said with pride. I wasn't expecting an answer. I was just talking in order to break the silence and to let her hear a friendly voice.

I picked up one of the books, crawled up on the bed next to her, and started to cradle her in my arms, to read to her. Her body suddenly got ridged. I felt a tugging at my heart. A child should feel reassured when an adult holds them. This child was fearful of human touch and I knew how that felt, yet I also knew that it felt good to be held in a loving manner with no strings attached. I felt a mixture of emotions at that point. I felt so bad for her, yet angry at whoever made her react this way. I finished putting my arm around her and spoke softly. "It's alright honey. I'm just going to read to you. Now let's see Pokey puppy use to be one of my favorites when I was your age." After a couple of minutes I could feel the little girl start to relax some and I kept right on reading.

Shortly after I started reading the lady with the book cart came by and I told her to keep me furnished with books, anything light hearted would do.

The little girl just lay there in my arms. At first she just stared at the ceiling then eventually she turned her attention to the books and seemed to be listening intently.

After several hours the little girl went to sleep, so I just stayed there talking softly to her, telling her stories about my children and stroking her hair. I was trying to radiate as much love as possible, without scaring her. Then Ned poked his head in the door and motioned me to the hallway. Slowly I worked my arm out from under the girl and tiptoed out to the hallway.

"Any luck," Ned asked as the door swung shot behind me.

"Ned, Have you talked to Doctor Jenkins," I asked.

Ned nodded his head with a look of rage on his face. "I want that son of a . . ." He didn't finish the sentence and just shuck his head.

I replied, "Me to, but I need to take this slow and easy with the kid. It's going to take time for her to learn to trust me." I told Ned what had happened earlier when I went to hold her.

Ned shock his head, "Damn, Ricky, I may have asked to much of you, but I'm more sure than ever that you're the one to help her."

"I'm in it now Ned and your not going to stop me," I replied as I wondered about his statement. "Now I need you to do me a favor and run past my daughter's house and ask her for these books and bring them back here to me." I wrote down a list of books that were mostly old classics like, *The Black Stallion* and *Lad the Dog*.

Ned looked confused, "Why do you want these books? Your suppose to be finding out who she is and where she came from."

"Ned, I can't get anything out of her if I can't get her to trust me enough to talk to me. Now don't tell me that you came by just to bust my chops."

Ned looked embarrassed, "I'm sorry Ricky, I know you're right." Then he changed the subject. "I wanted you to know that I ran the car and its came back stolen out of Washington State and the plates don't match the car. They came off from a car in Montana. If that girl in there doesn't tell us something we're in for a long haul."

"I'd say that they were on the run from someone, possibly the father." I was thinking out loud.

"Possibly," Ned replied, "but let's not jump to conclusions."

"I know, I know, stick to the facts. I'm just trying to think things through and consider all possibilities," I explained. "Now off with you and get those books." Ned nodded his head and started to walk away. "Ned," I called after him. He stopped and looked back at me. "Kyle is in the cafeteria waiting for me," I said. "Tell him not to bother I'm staying here with the kid tonight."

Just then a scream came from the hospital room. Ned and I both charged into the room, ready to pounce on whatever horrible creature had caused the girl to scream out in panic. The little girl was sitting up screaming at the top of her lungs, "I didn't mean to. I'll try harder I promise." She started bawling uncontrollably and repeating, "I'm sorry." Then she put up her arm in front of her face as though trying to shield it from an expected slap or something. I ran to the bed and swept the girl up into my arms and held her tightly. I kept saying, "It's okay honey. It's no big deal. We'll take care of it." She struggled with me at first as though she was fighting to get away. Finally she quieted down. The poor child was soaking wet, partly from perspiration, but mostly from urine. She had been so scared that when I picked her up she had wet herself. I sent Ned to get a clean gown and bedding from the nurse, then he slipped away quietly. After cleaning her up and changing the bed I laid her back down and started talking to her again as though nothing had happened. "Well sleepy head I see you woke up at last." I started adjusting her blankets and Pillows, as I talked on about anything that would come to me. My voice was shacking and tears started to fill my eyes as I fought them back, but I kept on talking until both her and I had settled back down.

Soon the girl and I had settled back to read another stack of books.

A couple of hours later Ned returned with the books I requested, some clean clothes for me and a note from my daughter. Ned most have explained the situation to her and being the concerned person she was she wrote this note:

> Mom,
> If you need someone to fill in for you at any time, call.
> All My Love,
> Annie

She had an idea there. If she came in and read to the girl I could go to Washington and Montana and check out the only leads we had to this girls past. Could I ask Annie to get involved? I didn't think I could expect her to deal with this situation. It was hard enough for me to understand. How could I ask Annie to? Granted, Annie was a Special Ed teacher and had a very special way with children that I never had. I was sure that she had seen some unusual case, but she was also married and had her husband to think about. I'd have to think all of this through carefully before deciding.

Meanwhile I would continue to read and talk to the girl for a while longer and hope for a break. After getting cleaned up and changing my clothes, I went back to reading. It did feel good to get the urine smell off from me.

Sometime in the middle of the night I drifted off to sleep, still holding the little girl in my arms. When I woke up at six o'clock the next morning my arm was asleep from the girl lying on it all night and I realized I hadn't eaten or had a cup of coffee since I left the Hitching Post the morning before. My stomach was letting me know that I had better put something in it soon.

I slid my arm out from under the little girl's head and rubbed it and flexed my fingers until the feeling returned. Then I slipped out of the room. Doctor Jenkins sent a nurse into the room to watch over the girl until I returned.

I stopped by my place to get refreshed and packed a few essentials. Then headed down the street toward the Hitching Post. Mrs. Wiggins' puppy met me for his morning scratch behind the ear and Ralph the taxi driver waved as he passed. Nothing had change out here, but something was changing inside of me and I could sense it.

As I walked to the Hitching Post I kept running the past twenty-four hours through my mind. My mind was reeling as millions of thoughts whirled around inside my head. This case had stirred something inside of me that I had thought had been laid to rest long ago. As I walked in the door Becky, Ned and Kyle turned to look at me in an expectant manner. I just shock my head and sat down at the counter.

Becky poured me a cup of coffee and stood over me as usual ready to pour again. "Long night huh Ricky."

I nodded my head. "Ya, it was.

"Ned told me about what has happened. Are you sure you're ready to deal with all this case entails?" Becky wasn't being nosy. She was just trying to make me think about what I had gotten into.

I thought about what she was saying for a moment then replied, "I have to be. I think this child needs constant attention, not just quick visits from the sterile, intellectual shrink, waiting to be lead around by the nose by social services." I never had been a great fan of state policies, when it came to children.

As a child my life was turned upside down, because some do-gooder felt the need to stick their nose in where it didn't belong. Then the state let it be known what they wanted my life to be. In my book they were dead wrong. After my mother died, Social Services believed that my father and brothers were incapable of raising me without the woman's influence they felt I needed, so I spend most of my live in an abusive foster home. Of course, once I was placed with this family, I was forgotten about. This child had already been through more than she deserved. I wasn't about to let anybody make a bad situation worse, if that was possible. Changing the subject I asked, "What's the special this morning?"

Ned spoke up, "Anything you want Ricky. It's on me."

Becky rebutted, "No! As long as you're working for the police department it's on the house, Jake said so." Then she poured another cup of coffee for me. I was sure that Becky new what was running through my mind and didn't bring up the subject of me bowing out again. Sometimes I had the feeling that Becky had a sixth sense, the way she read my thoughts, but maybe it was because down deep inside we were a lot alike.

"God, I guess I chose the wrong career field. I should have become a cop." I gave Becky a halfway grin. "I'll have ham and eggs, you know how I like them."

Becky nodded, wrote the ticket and placed it on the wheel. Jake looked through the window gave me a wink and started my order.

Turning back to me and constantly topping off my coffee, Becky asked, "Well what do you think? Are you making any headway?"

"I don't know, but I hope so," I replied. Then I turned to Ned. "Anything more on the car or the plates?"

"I've sent an inquiry to the police department in both towns, but I haven't gotten an answer back yet." I could tell he was frustrated.

I was too, but I knew that I had to be patient with the girl if I was to get anywhere.

We talked for a while as I ate my breakfast and downed several cups of coffee, then I tipped Becky, thanked her for her concern and left the Hitching Post.

Kyle followed me out the door. "Ricky, if you'd like I'll come over when I get off duty and read to the girl for a while."

I smiled at him and replied, "That's nice of you, but under the circumstances I'm not sure that's a good idea, at least not yet."

Kyle nodded sadly and said, "Ya, I guess your right. The poor little thing probably isn't real secure around men right now."

"It was a nice gesture though and you're a sweetheart for suggesting it." I felt sorry for him. He wanted so much to help and didn't know how. I wasn't sure how any of us could help that little girl. At the moment I was just going on instinct.

Remembering my mental note from the day before, about reassuring Kyle, I said, "Once I get some answers you'll be able to be a big part of this investigation, I'm sure."

He smiled, "Ya, I'm sure you're right." He appeared to be pleased with that thought as he said, "then we can nail that piece of trash."

"That's a day we can all look forward to," I answered. Then I left Kyle and went back to the hospital to continue working with the girl.

That evening Ned stopped by to see how things were going and we went to the cafeteria to talk.

"So how's it going Ricky," he asked, sure that he already knew the answer.

"She seems a little less tense, but that's about all," I replied.

"Ricky," Ned said in an apprehensive manner, "I'm not sure, but I think I may have stirred up a hornet's nest."

"What do you mean," I asked.

"Well, I ran the woman's prints through the data bank and a hold from the Feds flashed up on the screen."

I sat up in my chair, "Oh really," I remarked. Ned had definitely grabbed my attention. "What do you make of that?"

"I'm not sure," Ned replied, "But I guess we'll be getting visitors very soon. I'm just not sure if that's good or bad."

"Well," I replied, as I got to my feet. "I better get back to the girl. We may not have much time."

After spending a week with the girl I was running out of things to say and my eyes were getting bloodshot from reading. One night while I was straightening her pillow she looked right at me and said, "Where's Mama?"

At first I stopped in my tracks out of shock that she had spoken. Then it hit me what she had asked. How was I to tell her that her mother was dead? As it turned out I didn't exactly have to tell her, because as I was trying to chose my words she said, "Mama's dead isn't she?" She looked so mature for a child her age, that it almost spooked me.

"Yes honey, she is, but don't you worry. You're fine and your safe." I didn't know at that point whether to tell her I would find her family or that I would protect her, because I didn't know the whole story yet. "Can you tell me your name?"

She looked nervous. "I'm not suppose to tell anyone."

"Who told you not to tell," I asked. She picked up a teddy bear and hugged onto it for dear life. She was trembling. I placed my hand on her shoulder and she flinched and stiffened up. "It's okay honey. Just lie down and relax." Suddenly she looked at me with total dread written all over her face. Then with trembling hands she removed her gown and panties. I was puzzled. What was she doing? Then the tiny little girl lay back on the bed and slowly bent her knees and started spreading her legs apart as she stared at the ceiling, still trembling. I stood there in shock. Then I noticed tears seeping out of the corners of her eyes as she uttered, in what seemed to be an almost hypnotic state, yet her voice was breaking up, "I'll try to do be good this time, I promise." Then I could see every muscle in her body tighten up as she pinched her eyes closed tightly and gritted her teeth. I could tell she was expecting the force and excruciating pain that should come next.

I could feel my knees trying to buckle out from under me as I struggled to remain strong. "Oh my god," I said. I was shaking uncontrollably as I reached down and pulled the covers over her. "Honey you don't ever have to do that again." I was choking back the tears as I turned away from her to regain my composure.

Just then I spotted Becky standing in the doorway holding a tray of food. The look on her face told me that she was as horrified as I was. She must have sensed that I was about to lose total control, because she sat the tray down quickly, grabbed me firmly by the shoulders and shook me, as she said, "I'll take over here Ricky. Get out of here for a minute and when you're able, go get Dr. Jenkins."

My eyes were starting to water and I felt as though I was freezing cold. I looked at Becky and said, "How could . . ."

I could have sworn for a split second there that a look of terror had appeared on Becky's face then she gave me another quick shake and her expression changed to that of determination, as she said in a forceful manner, "Ricky, go!"

I nodded my understanding and stumbled out of the room. With each step I felt overwhelming rage boil up inside of me in a way I hadn't felt for a very long time.

Chapter Five

As I walked down the hallway of the hospital, that day I felt my head start to spin. I staggered to a chair and sat down and buried my head in my hands. That poor child, having to live through such a thing. This is a sick world we live in, I thought to myself. I was shaking uncontrollably and cussing to myself.

Suddenly I felt somebody's hands on mine. I looked up to see Dr. Jenkins kneeling down in front of me and looking sympathetic. "Getting tired Ricky?"

"It's not that Doc. I want to slice and dice the bastard that did this to that poor little girl in there." I nodded my head in the direction of the little girl's room. The rage had boiled up inside of me to the point that I wanted to hit something and wasn't real choosy about what or who.

Dr. Jenkins spoke in a calm steady tone; "You have to be strong if you really want to do this. Things are going to happen with her that are hard to deal with."

I braced myself and said, "I'm sorry Doc, but I can't help the fact that I want this person's head mounted on a dart board."

"I know Ricky, but right now that girl needs help." He paused for a moment and I could tell by the look on his face that he really did know. Then he said, "Are you ready to tell me what happened?"

"Oh, Doc it's enough to make your stomach churn." I replied.

"I think I know what you're getting at. Believe me Ricky, in this business I've seen it all. Not much surprises me anymore. It doesn't make me happy by any means, but it doesn't surprise me either."

After a few minutes of threats and cuss words, I told Jenkins what happened. He just nodded as though he had expected it.

"Ricky that's not unusual. I think it's time that I give you some information so you know what you're up against, but right now she needs to know that she hasn't been rejected by you for what she has done. Do you think you're ready to go back in there?"

I took a deep breath and nodded my head. "Let's do this," I said through gritted teeth, but I'm telling you Doc, as soon as it's safe to leave her, I'm going after the bastard that did this to her!"

"I know Ricky," he replied, "I know, but remember to be absolutely sure of all the facts before you act. Believe me, cases like this can be very deceiving." He stopped walking, turned, took me by the shoulders and looked straight into my eyes. "Also Ricky, don't let this eat at you until you lose all sense of right and wrong. It's your job to find the creep. It's the law's job to deal with him."

"I'll try Doc," I replied.

He gave me a warning look then, then asked, "Are you ready?"

I took a deep breath and released it then nodded and we both stepped back into the little girl's room. Becky was sitting by the bed watching the little girl sleep, when we returned. She looked up and whispered, "Ricky, she's sleeping now, let's go for a walk." I could tell that what she had witnessed when she walked in had broken her heart as much as it infuriated me.

Doctor Jenkins whispered, "I think that's a good idea. I'll make sure she's alright while your gone."

I nodded and Becky and I left the room. As we walked to the elevator Becky was very quiet, but I could tell that she was studying me. We rode the elevator to the ground floor and stepped out into the garden area that the hospital had neatly arranged. Just as we walked out through the automatic glass doors, to our right was a small coffee stand with a glass case, which held cookies, sweet rolls and other snacks. There were several trees for shade and neatly trimmed hedges that stood about four feet high, which lined the walkways. Each walkway wound around the garden area and ended up back at the beginning again. Scattered around the grassy areas encircled by the hedge-lined walkways, there were metal patio tables and chairs, with huge umbrellas shading each one.

We walked over to a patio table and sat down. Becky just sat across the table from me and waited for me to speak. I didn't know what to say without sounding like a murderous maniac, so I said, "Want some coffee or something?"

Becky shook her head, "No thanks." Then she reached out and placed a caring hand over mine, which were clasped tightly in front of me on the table. "Ricky, this is unbelievable. What are you going to do?"

"I'm not sure," I replied. "I'm in a pickle. I need to get out there and find the girl's family and the monster that did this to her, yet I can't just leave her." I paused a moment. I was trying to sound professional and unshaken as I continued, "I know it looked bad up there just now, but I think I'm finally getting through to her too. I'm not sure if it's wise to leave her right now. Annie offered to come in and watch her for me, but I sure can't ask her to deal with this."

Becky looked edgy. She took a deep breath as though preparing for the worst and said, "How about me?"

I shook my head, "Oh Becky, I can't ask anyone to deal with this but me right now. I'm the one that she has been with since the beginning I have to stick with it for now, until she feels safe enough with someone else to speak to them."

Becky seemed relieved with my answer as she replied, "You're probably right, but I thought I'd offer anyway."

Becky had hinted in the past that she had been sexually abused when she was younger and I couldn't ask her to relive that part of her life. I had already had to start confronting my past with this case, although I wasn't about to admit it to anyone. I too had been molested when I was a little younger then this child until I was about ten. Not to the extent that this child had, but I was still ashamed whenever I let myself think about it. No matter how often a person is told that it wasn't their fault the shame is always there.

Becky and I talked for a while longer until I was ready to face the situation again, then we returned to the room.

My son, Jesse was home on summer break from college, by now and had stopped by the hospital to check on me. When he stepped into the room he spotted the little girl sitting on the bed looking confused and a nurse sitting in a chair reading a book. When Jesse stepped in the nurse looked up. "You must be Ricky's son."

Jesse nodded, but never took his eyes off from the girl.

The nurse continued, "She talks a lot about you and your sister. She should be back soon."

Jesse replied, "I'll wait." His focus was on the girl in the bed staring back at him.

The little girl looked nervous as she stared at Jesse. Jesse sensing this smiled then looked down on the floor, as he got a curious look on his face. Then he got down on his hands and knees and appeared to be studying something on the floor.

The little girl's curiosity got the better of her and she leaned over the edge of the bed to see what Jesse was doing. Knowing now that he had her undivided attention, Jesse reached out and appeared to be slowly picking something up off from the floor and studying it, but the girl saw nothing in his hand. Then as though something had yanked on him, Jesse did a backward flip and staggered to his feet appearing to be pulling hard on something. Then he pulled what ever it was toward the girl and said, "Could you hold my elephant for me . . . ?" He looked at the girl as though expecting an answer to an unasked question.

"Penny," she replied without thinking.

"Could you hold my elephant for me Penny, while I tie my shoe?" He now had a pleading look on his face.

Penny nodded. She was more than willing to play along.

Jesse pretended to tie his shoe then thanked her and took the make believe rope back from Penny. He held out his hand. With a wide, goofy smile on his face he said, "My name is Jesse. Glad to meet you Penny."

Penny laughed and shook his hand.

Just then Jesse fell backward with a jerk and landed stretch up on his back on the floor. He staggered to his feet again, as though wrestling to get his imaginary elephant under control.

Just then Becky and I walked into the room and I got a major shock. I saw my son clowning around, doing his silly little pantomime about trying to lead an elephant on a rope and the girl was sitting up on the bed and giggling as she watched him. Jesse had always been able to make little kids laugh, but I never thought this little girl would be comfortable with a young man, especially one as big as Jesse was. He was a very big eighteen-year-old. He stood six feet two inches tall and weighed two hundred and fifty pounds. His hands were twice the size of mine and a person would think he'd scare this little girl to death, but she seemed very comfortable around him. When he spotted me, he said, "Hi mom, Penny and I were just getting to know each other."

My mouth dropped open in surprise. "How did you find out her name was Penny?" I couldn't believe it. Jesse had found out her name in just a few minutes. I was glad, but totally confused. This little girl should have been scared to death of Jesse, but she took right to him. Every other male that had come near her had made her freeze up, even Doc Jenkins to a point. Was it that he just started right in clowning around with her or was it more? Whatever it was would come to me in time, but for now I was just thankful.

Jesse smiled at me in a goofy, but proud way and said, "She told me."

I looked back and forth between the two of them. "Well, does Penny have a last name?"

Jesse stuck a little red ball on the end of his nose, crossed his eyes and stuck his tongue out the side of his mouth. Then he said, talking around his tongue "Well of course she has a last name. We just haven't gotten to that yet, but if you're a good little girl and go with this young lady and get something warm to eat," he motioned toward Becky, "and tuck yourself into bed and say you're prays, we might have a surprise for you by morning."

Penny laughed at Jesse's every move. I wasn't sure about leaving Penny and Jesse alone all night. What if she suddenly did something like she did earlier? Jesse would come unglued, worse than I did. I knew my son. His love for little children and his overwhelming need for justice would be more powerful then his new-found maturity would be able to handle.

Dr. Jenkins had followed Becky and I into the room and was watching the whole thing. He must have been reading my mind, because he stepped up and said, "We've got him covered Ricky. I think you've found your solution."

"Maybe," I replied tentatively.

Becky grabbed my arm. "Come on Ricky, let's go."

I walked over to Penny and asked, "Do you mind if Jesse stays with you tonight?"

She just smiled a big smile and replied, "I'd like that."

I was totally befuddled, but nodded and left the room. As Becky and I walked I tried to sort out what had just happened, but nothing made any sense.

On our way to the Hitching Post Becky watched my reaction for a while then said, "You know Jesse might just be the answer to your prayers."

I nodded and replied, "Maybe, but what about the other stuff? Jesse is very softhearted and wants to save the world. How will he handle Penny's little episodes?"

"We'll all keep an eye on him. Besides you were wondering who could get close enough to her to get her to open up and Jesse has done that. He'd be good for her. He can show her that not all men are cruel."

As we stepped inside the Hitching Post I replied, "Well he is on summer break from college. Okay, you're probably right. I'll check it out with him tomorrow."

Kyle was sitting at the counter when Becky and I stepped inside and took a table by the door. He stood up when he saw us and walked over to our table. "May I join you ladies."

"Sure Kyle," I replied. "I need to talk to the police department anyway."

As he sat down he said, "Well, I'm not exactly the police department, but what did you need?"

"I'd like your sketch artist to make me a drawing of Penny's mother, as she would have looked when she was alive," I answered. "I don't want to be showing around a morgue picture of her. Besides I'm not sure I want anyone to know that she's dead yet."

"Penny!" Kyle was surprised. "Well Ricky you finally did it. That's great!"

"Actually it was Jesse that got her to tell her name," I declared. "He's working on a last name right now."

Kyle was even more amazed, "Jesse!"

"I know Kyle," I responded to his reaction. "It shocked me too. I would have never guessed that she would open up to any male, but I was wrong. Maybe I should have let you try."

Becky spoke up. "No offense Kyle, but I think for some reason it had to be Jesse."

Kyle and I both looked at Becky. "Why?"

Becky replied, "I don't know. I think that Penny sees something in Jesse that she can relate to. I'm not sure what, but there's something there. Maybe it's the little boy in him."

"That's got to be it Becky." I had to admit that Beck might have hit the nail right on the head. I had to chuckle just a bit though, to think of my big son and realize that there is still a lot of little boy in him.

"Anyway," I turned back to Kyle, "Is there a chance of having that picture done by tomorrow afternoon."

Kyle stood up, "I'll get right on it Ricky." I could tell that he was glad to finally be able to do something to help. "I'll update the Chief for you, while I'm at it."

I thanked him and he left to carry out my wishes.

Chapter Six

After Kyle had left, Becky suddenly became a waitress again and stated, "Now, it's time to get some real food into you and take you home. You need to be sharp for tomorrow."

"You're right as usual. I can't afford to make any mistakes from here on out. That kids safety depends on what I do next." I tried not to let my insecurities show as I spoke. I only hoped I had what it took to do this job right.

Becky stood up to place an order with the cook personally as she looked at me in a knowing manner, "You'll know what to do when the time comes Ricky. I know you. You have an insight to this case that nobody else here has." Becky seemed to sense my past, but never came right out and said it. I had to think that we were more alike than either of us would admit. We just seemed to know what the other one had been through.

Becky turned and walked to the kitchen. I didn't have to tell her what I wanted to eat. She always knew just by my moods what I would order. When she returned to the table with my coffee she said, "Your order will be here in a few minutes." She sat back down and said, "I called Annie and explained the whole situation to her. She insisted that she would check in on Jesse and Penny often."

Annie had a special bond with her brother. Like most big sisters she picked on him most of the time, but her love for him was deeper than he would ever suspect. She would give her life to keep any harm from coming to him, and course he would do the same for her too. Jesse was twice his sister's size, but Annie was a scrapper when the need arose. Annie was the stable one of the three of us. She was a school teacher and lived a proper life, but when she was riled up, she would shock everyone around her as she ripped her antagonist to shreds, then calmly convert back to her proper self in the blink of an eye. I've witnessed it with my own two eyes and even though I am her mother, I still have a hard time believing it.

"That's good," I replied, "She'll be able to pack him down if he needs it. Nobody else will be able to deal with his rage if Penny should do anything like what she did tonight. You think I was angry! You've never seen Jesse when he wants to stop someone's pain."

"We'll all keep that in mind, Ricky. You just worry about what you have to do," Becky assured me. Just then the food arrived. I hadn't realized just how hungry I was until that moment. Becky and I ate, drank coffee and laid out the plans for the next day. Finally she dropped me off at my place and ordered me to get a good night's rest.

I lay on my couch that night staring at the ceiling. I had a mixture of emotions. I felt a bit of excitement thinking about starting my investigation. I could finally be doing something worth while. Maybe I could even deal with my own past, by helping Penny. I hoped that I didn't end up hurting her chances to be happy. I had to be sure that I didn't hand her over to the wrong person. I knew that many abuses occur within the family, but how would I find out which family member was safe, if any. Her mother obviously was running from something. Was it her whole family? Was it because of Penny's abuse or something else all together? After a while I drifted off to sleep.

When I walked into the Hitching Post the next morning Ned and Kyle were waiting for me. Ned handed me a folder as Becky poured my coffee and nodded toward Jake. She turned back to me and said, "Breakfast is on the way."

I smiled, "Boy, suddenly I feel like a young kid on my way of to my first day of college and getting the VIP treatment."

Ned replied, "We just want to make sure you have everything you need to find out the truth about that poor little girl, Ricky."

"I know Ned and I'll try my best not to let you or her down." I was nervous but anxious at the same time. At last I was going after the sorry excuse for a human being that caused all of the pain to that little girl.

"I know you will Ricky, but don't let your anger cloud your judgment." Ned was worried. I could tell by the tone of his voice.

"Don't worry Ned. I'll watch my temper. I know I have to be absolutely sure of what happened. I also know it's not my job to play judge and jury, but it will give me great satisfaction in putting the reptile away." Then I quickly changed the subject. "So let's see what you've got in here for me." I opened the folder and pulled out the papers inside. There was all the information on the car and license plate. Also there was a picture of Penny and a computer image of her mother. "Wow, that's a great picture."

Kyle spoke with pride. "Isn't it amazing what can be done with computers these days."

"Yes it is Kyle." Just then breakfast arrived and I put everything back into the folder. "Now I have everything I need for my trip." I ate my breakfast. Then as I prepared to leave. I reminded everybody to watch Jesse and Penny and said that I was going by the hospital before I left.

I walked into the hospital room to see Jesse asleep in a chair in the corner and Penny sleeping soundly in her bed. I reached down and lightly shook Jesse. He rubbed his eyes then focused on me. Then he motioned toward the hallway. Once outside I asked him how the night went.

Jesse shook his head. "She had a rough one mom, but I got a couple of last names out of her. I've written them down for you. I think she's been forced to change her name a lot of times, but I think the real one is Johnson."

I did my best to make Penny's condition clear to Jesse and to warn him not to lose control, because Penny needed his strength. He said he understood. I gave him a hug and said, "you've turned into a wonderful young man and I'm proud of you son."

Jesse smiled proudly and said, "Thanks mom and don't worry. We'll be fine. Just get that creep."

"I'll certainly try," I replied then I left the hospital.

I could feel a surge of adrenaline as I reached for the door handle of my car and prepared to leave for Montana. Just then I heard Ned calling to me. "Ricky, hold on a minute."

I turned to see Ned and a middle aged man walking my way.

I froze in my tracks. I'd never seen this man before. He was tall, about six feet three or four inches. He had dark hair and walked as though he was marching in a parade. It was almost a strut. Could this be somebody from Penny's family? *No Ricky, don't react. Just listen and don't show your hand until you are sure that you know the truth.* I stood there trying to look calm as they approached.

Ned looked nervous and displeased. "Ricky, this is Cody Hicks of the U.S. Marshal's office. He'd like to talk to you about Penny." Ned spoke as though he had a bad taste in his mouth.

Deputy Marshal Hick's reached out and shook my hand. "Mrs . . ."

I interrupted. "Ricky, just Ricky."

The Marshal smiled, "Ricky, I understand that you are looking into the origin of this young lady." He showed me a picture of Penny.

"What about it?" I had a feeling that I wouldn't like where this was leading. I thought to myself. Well, Ned was right. We got a visitor and it didn't take very long.

"Well the Marshal's office is taking over this case, but thank you for your concerns," Hicks answered.

"Isn't this case a little beneath the Marshal's office?"

"I can't get into it with you right now. I'm just telling you to drop the case. We have it under control and all you can do is get in the way."

I glanced at Ned. He was giving me a look that was telling me not to admit anything, so I said. "That's fine with me. I was just on my way to visit relatives in Ohio anyway. My son is sitting with the girl. She has taken a liking to him, so I feel free to go now. I hope you get what you're looking for."

Ned gave a knowing grin and added, "and don't forget to give my best to your Uncle Harry and tell him to come visit soon."

"I will Ned." Then I turned to Marshal Hicks. "Well I'm glad you're on the case. I can breath freely now. Good luck and nice meeting you."

The Deputy Marshal didn't look quite convinced as he said. "Nice meeting you too."

I started the engine and pulled away, as I mumbled to myself, "Drop the case my butt! Who does this guy think he is?"

Chapter Seven

As I reached the interstate an old feeling came over me. When I was younger I traveled the highways a lot. I enjoyed talking on the CB to the truckers and seeing the sights. As I got older I started worrying more and more about earning enough to support the kids. I got lost in day to day life. I wouldn't have traded those years with my kids for anything, but they were grown now and it was kind of nice to be on the road again. For a while I forgot about the case and just drove west, enjoying the sights. I almost wished that I had a CB.

After a while I came back to reality and concentrated on the reason I was out there to begin with. I drove most of the day then finally my stomach started growling so I started looking for some place to stop.

Eventually I spotted a sign that said there was a truck stop at exit 9A around Gary Indiana. I got off at that exit. When I settled at a table, I started looking over the information in the folder. I couldn't get my mind off from Deputy Marshal Hicks telling me to drop the case. He didn't even have any questions for me. That struck me as odd. After all, I was the one that had been with Penny since her sudden arrival in our little town. I would have thought he would want to talk to me about what I knew, but instead he just blew me off.

I didn't know whether to be angry or suspicion. What did the U.S. Marshal's office have to do with Penny and her mother? I told myself that I would have to find a library somewhere and find out more about the duties of the U.S. Marshal's office. All I really knew about them was that they transported federal prisoners. I really didn't believe that Penny's mother was an escape federal prisoner. I don't know why I was so sure of that, but I was.

As I sat there looking over the papers and thinking about the case, the waitress came by my table to fill my coffee cup and take my order. When she saw what I was looking at, she inquired, "Do you know Lilly?"

I was totally confused by that question. Who was this Lilly person and why was this waitress asking me if I knew her? I looked up at the waitress. Her name tag said Patty. She was probably in her thirties; about five foot seven of eight, slender built with short brown hair.

"What?" I responded to her question the only way I could think of, until I knew what she was getting at.

Then Patty pointed to the picture of Penny's mother and said, "Lilly. Do you know her?" Then she stepped back a bit and covered her mouth with her hand as though she shouldn't have said anything.

"No," I answered, "but I know her daughter Penny." I showed her the picture of Penny, then asked, "How did you know them?"

She seemed to be covering for blurting out Lilly's identity as she said, "I'm sorry that's not Lilly. It just looked a little like her. As for the kid, I've never seen her before."

"Look Patty is it? I'm not out to hurt anybody, least of all Lilly." I was sure that she was hiding something and I had to convince her that I wasn't any danger. "I represent this child."

"I didn't know that there was a little girl." She seems surprised at hearing about Lilly having a child. "I just met Lilly." Patty hesitated for a while, then said, "She worked here for a week, then disappeared the minute she got paid."

"She never mentioned her daughter?" I asked.

"No, she didn't."

"Please it's important that I find out about this woman, for the girls sake." I was picking my words carefully and so was she.

"She sure was a nervous thing. She jumped at every little noise." Patty replied. Then she fidgeted as she poured my coffee and took my order. Just before she left my table she said, "That Lilly's got a major problem that's for sure."

I didn't want to ask too many questions right then and scare Patty off or attract any unwanted attention so I just nodded my head and let her be on her way for the moment. The next time that she came back to the table I asked, "Would it be possible for me to talk to you about Lilly when you get off work?"

"I suppose so," she replied. She still seemed nervous as she almost whispered, "meet me in the parking lot in about an hour.

I nodded my understanding and let her go about her business.

That next hour I sat and drank coffee, ate my meal and tried not to look interested in much of anything. When I was sure that it was getting close to time for Patty to leave, I paid my bill, left a tip and headed outside. I poked around in the trunk of my car as though I was looking for something, until she showed up.

She walked over to me and said, "I don't know if I should talk to you. I don't know what kind of trouble Lilly was in and I don't want to cause her any more problems."

I shook my head, "Believe me you won't cause her any more trouble." I didn't want to volunteer too much information, so I repeated to her what I had stated inside, "I'm just trying to help Penny and I need to know more about Lilly, in order to do that. Do you know what kind of trouble Lilly was in?"

"No," She replied, "She did mention that she hadn't done anything illegal, but she always seemed to avoid the police. She'd say things like, 'you never know which ones to trust.' That didn't make any sense to me."

"That is strange," I replied. It sounds to me as though she had run into some dirty cops in the past."

"That's all I could figure from the way she acted," Patty agreed.

Do you know where she stayed or if she talked to anybody, while she was here," I asked. I knew that I was probably grasping at straws.

She shook her head, "I think she stayed in our lodging. I don't remember her car leaving the parking lot very often. I asked her a couple of times if she'd like to come home with me, but she always said she had things to attend to."

I nodded my acknowledgment, "Yah, Penny."

She shook her head in disbelief, "Evidently. She seemed very nice, but something had her very scared too. She stayed to herself most of the time, as though she was afraid someone might recognize her or find out too much about her."

"Why do you suppose that she didn't stick around."

Patty got a thoughtful look on her face and replied, "The day that Lilly left, two guys came in. I'm not sure, but it seemed to me that they were watching her every move. I mentioned it to Lilly and I asked her if she knew them. She said that she didn't, but they did make her nervous. Suddenly she spoke to the boss, got her pay and slipped out the back door."

What did these two guys look like, I asked.

She thought for a moment then said, "From what I remember they were sort of the Mutt and Jeff types. You know, one tall and skinny and one short and chubby."

"Anything else," I asked.

"Not that I can think of," She answered. "I'm not real good at faces, but I know they creeped me out."

I reached out and shook Patty's hand, "Thank you for talking to me. By the way, has anybody else come around asking any questions about her?"

"The U.S. Marshal's office seems terribly interested in her. I've had two different Deputy Marshals ask about her."

I stiffened up. "What did you tell them," I asked.

"I didn't tell them anything. I know I probably should have, but I didn't know what to do and Lilly was so afraid of the police."

"That was probably wise," I replied. "I still haven't figured out their tie in all of this, but until I do, I'm like Lilly. I don't trust anybody."

"Just how do you tie into all of this," Patty asked.

"I have Penny, or at least I know where she is, but I don't know where she came from. I just want to help her be somewhere that's safe. At this point I'm not sure where that is." I studied Patty's expression. She seemed to care what happened to Lilly. I asked, "By the way, not that it's right, but what did Lilly give for a last name?"

"Peter's, why?"

"Just wondering," I said, as I looked at the list of last names Jesse had given me at the hospital. "Do me a favor. Don't tell anyone about seeing me, especially not the U.S. Marshals. They don't want me involved."

She nodded her head. "Okay, I hope you find what you're looking for. I'd hate to see any kid be lost and alone."

I thanked her and got into my car, "One more thing, do you know of some place where I can park my car and get some sleep for the night?"

"There is a place for RV's over there." She pointed in the direction of several RV's. "I wouldn't advice staying here in lodging. It's too busy if you know what I mean."

I chuckled, "Yes I think I do. Thanks again."

She added, "by the way we have private showers here if you need one. The truckers use them when they're on their long hauls."

"Thanks," I replied as I started my car and headed over to where the RV's were parked.

Once I found a safe looking place to park where I didn't think I'd be spotted very easily, I turned on my dome light and jotted down all the information the waitress had given me. Peters was one of the names on Jesse's list, but I was pretty sure that wasn't her real name. I wasn't even sure that Lilly was her real name. The one thing I was sure of was that I would have to be extra careful. The Marshals were unmistakably involved, but how? Lilly, or whoever she was, did not trust the law, but why? I still had more questions than answers. I definitely hoped that Hicks had bought my story about visiting relatives.

As I reclined my seat back, I planned out what I would have to do the next day. *In the morning I need to call Westfield. I need to check on Jesse and Penny and I need to update Ned, but what if Hicks is still hanging around? I guess I could call Becky at the Hitching Post. I doubt that Hicks would think of me calling there. I also need to find a library and hopefully figure out what there is about Penny and Lilly that the Marshals could be so interested in. After that I will check out other truck stops on my way to Montana. I'm getting the feeling that Lilly, or whoever she was, might have frequented truck stops. Then what was she doing in Westfield? It's quite a ways from the freeway.* Finally I nodded off to sleep.

I woke up a couple of hours later, stiff and sore. I was not going to get comfortable in that seat again and I knew it, so I climbed over to the back seat and curl up for a couple of more hours. About four o'clock in the morning I gave up and walked around for a while to work the kinks out. Then I went to the showers to clear up. As I stood there letting the water rush over my stiff body, I reminded myself of what I needed to accomplish for the day. After my shower, I forced myself to get back into my car and back onto the freeway, headed west. I wasn't sure that I should return to that particular truck stop. I wanted to keep moving. I didn't want anyone to catch up with me that might try to stop me from finding out about Penny's past. I wanted to get some coffee. I would wait for another truck stop though, because I was hoping to get some more information at the same time.

Chapter Eight

After a while at South Beloit, Illinois I spotted another Truck stop. I hoped I'd get an indication soon on weather to take interstate 90 or 94. I wanted to follow Lilly's path if possible.

I needed to check in with Becky then get some breakfast. There was a line of pay phones just inside the door of the restaurant, so I picked up the receiver and punched in my code for my calling card then the number for the Hitching Post.

Jake answered the phone. "Hitching Post."

"Hi Jake, I'm sorry to bother you, but is Becky busy?"

"You might say that she's got company, but I'll call her back to the office and cover for her at the counter. There is only two people here right now, if you know what I mean."

"Thanks Jake." *That must mean that Deputy Marshal Hicks and someone else, I'd say probably Ned, was there. Hicks probably isn't letting Ned out of his sight.*

When Becky got to the phone she said, "Ricky, are you there?"

"Yes Becky. What's happening back there," I asked.

"Right now Hicks is out here with Ned, She spoke in a low tone so her voice wouldn't carry very far. "I think he's trying to get an indication from Ned about whether you really are at your uncles or not."

"So He's sticking around, I take it," I commented.

"Yes I'd say so," Becky answered.

"What else is going on, I asked. How about the kids? Is Jesse handling thing alright?"

"The kids are okay so far, but Jesse would really like to be doing what you're doing right now. He's building up quite a hatred for whoever did this to Penny." Becky paused for a second or two then continued. "She is still doing strange things that indicate that she's been sexually abused. She's acting it out still and she believes that people are displeased with her."

"Doctor Jenkins said that would happen, when he spoke to me at the hospital," I commented.

"Penny is still relating to Jesse very well though," Becky added, "and Annie has checked in a couple of time already. She's managed to convince Jesse, so far that he needs to stay here and work with Penny."

"That's right. He does," I replied.

"I hope Jesse never gets his hands on whoever did this to Penny." Becky continued. "There's no telling what he'd do, but I'm sure it wouldn't be pretty. Also Ricky, Jesse says that he's sure that Johnson is the right name."

"I'll remember that," I answered.

"Now how is it going with you," Becky asked.

I updated Becky and asked, "Can you try to find a way to tell Ned, without giving Hicks a hint of what's going on?"

"Not a problem Ricky. We've got quite a network going here." Becky chuckled.

"One more thing Becky." I said, "Tell the kids that I'm proud of them and for Jesse to hang in there. He's more help to me than he knows right where he is."

I will," Becky replied.

"What he gets from Penny could be the most valuable clues I get," I added. "Tell him that if he really wants this creep caught that what he's doing is essential to reach that goal."

"Okay, but Ricky, you better know, Hicks has an officer posted outside Penny's room all the time. Nothing can be said without the officer over hearing it."

Interesting! Becky, be careful. Don't say anything within earshot of that officer."

"Gotcha, Ricky."

"Okay," I said, "I've got to go. I'll call again tomorrow."

"Ricky, to play it safe, call me at home."

"Okay good-bye and thanks," I replied.

"Good-bye and be careful," Becky sounded worried.

"I will." I hung up the phone.

After hanging up I looked around the truck stop. It was fairly quiet. There were a few sleepy looking truck drivers scattered around at the tables. Four very loud teenagers at one table tossing french fries at each other and using language that would curl your hair. I shook my head and decided to sit at the counter, as far away from the noise as I could get.

I walked up to the counter of the restaurant and sat down, placing the folder on the counter in front of me. There were a couple of truck drivers sitting there harmlessly flirting with the waitress. "Honestly Phyllis, you're even sexier looking than usual. Don't you think so Frog?"

"No doubt about it, Creeper," the other driver said. I figured they had to be using CB handles. I would certainly hope so anyway. I'd hate to think that anybody would name his or her children Creeper and Frog.

Phyllis grinned and shook her head. "You two are so full of it, but don't stop. I like it. It makes my head swell even if you are full of it."

Frog smiled, "Aw Phyllis, you cut me to the quick."

Phyllis smiled and patted the top of his head and said, "Poor baby, I'm so sorry," and Creeper laughed.

Just then another trucker stepped up to the counter. "Are these lunkheads giving you a hard time this morning, Phyllis?"

Frog turned and said, "What's up guy? Haven't heard you on the box for a while."

"I've been doing short runs between Madison and Indianapolis lately, but I've got a West Coast run on right now. I thought I might give the Mariner and his little lady a yell while I'm out there."

Creeper grinned, "First he gets nervous Lilly a job at the truck stop, then he gets the run that just happens to take him by there several times a week. I'd say he's got the hots for her. Tell the Mariner that you need your head checked while you're out there."

That statement peaked my interest. I stared at my cup, but listened closely as they continued their conversation.

Frog added, "You don't happen to need to stop in Gary on these trips do you?" He chuckled and elbowed Creeper.

The driver's face turn slightly red and replied, "Lilly only stayed for a little while, then disappeared. By the way did you hear that Patty got jumped in the parking lot last night?"

Creeper spoke up with deep concern, "Is she alright?"

"She got roughed up pretty good, but she alright," The driver explained

"Why would anyone want to rough up Patty," Creeper asked.

"She's not saying anything about it, but I hear she was seen talking to a lady in the parking lot just before that. Then Patty went back inside for a while and when she left two guys jumped her," The driver continued. "If a Roadway driver hadn't have come along when he did, who knows what would have happened."

"Did they catch the two guys?"

"No, not yet. They ran when the Roadway driver yelled."

Frog turned to Phyllis. "You better have someone walk you to your car when you get off. Who knows where these sicko's will hit next."

Patty was the name of the waitress that I had spoken to the night before. Could these men have jumped her because of our meeting in the parking lot? This case was getting stranger by the minute. I had to wonder if these two men where the same two that showed up the night that Lilly took off. I must have parked far enough away that I didn't hear the ruckus. Patty could have given me up, but she must not have. For this I was grateful, but I felt badly for her getting ruffed up.

I wanted to talk to the driver, but I didn't think this was the time or place. I'd have to hang around a while and try to catch him alone. I got up and left a tip, paid for my coffee and hung around the game room, while I watched him out on the corner of my eye.

The teenagers got up and paid their bill while laughing and shoving each other. Phyllis remained polite, but I could tell by the look on her face that she couldn't wait for them to leave. After they left she went to clean up their mess.

I wandered through the game room watching some of the people play. I was starting to feel conspicuous, so I played a little too.

After some time, I noticed the truck driver pick up his ticket and reach for his wallet, so I stepped outside and waited for him.

When he stepped outside I said, "Excuse me sir, can I talk to you for a minute." He seemed to stand about six foot three or four. He had massive arms and a stocky build. He had a very dark tan, which seemed to highlight the bone structure of his face. It looked as though he could do some pretty serious damage to a person if he had a mind to, but he put off an air of kindness. It was nothing that I could put my finger on, but I instantly felt safe around him.

He smiled and replied, "How can I help you little lady?"

I showed him the picture of Lilly. "I'd like to ask you a few questions about this woman."

He stiffened up. "What about her?"

I could tell he was ready to defend her, so I said, "It's alright. I'm taking care of her daughter and just want to help, but I must warn you that I was the lady Patty was talking to in the parking lot lastnight. I hope that our conversation didn't have anything to do with her assault. She was very nice, but she seemed worried about talking to me."

He nodded as though he understood, "That's very possible." Then he pointed to the picture. "What do you want to know about Lilly?"

"Where did you meet her," I asked.

"In Fargo," he replied, "She was very nervous and looking for a job. She needed to make some quick money to keep moving. She was afraid of someone catching up with her. I assumed that she was running from an abusive relationship and whoever was after her had very powerful connections, maybe her husband or possessive boyfriend. So, knowing that Patty had said they needed another waitress, I told her that I'd put in a good word for her if she was headed that way."

I pulled out the picture of Penny and asked, "did you see this little girl with her?"

He looked at Penny's picture. "She's a cute little thing. Is this Lilly's daughter?"

"Yes she is. I take it you never saw her." I commented.

"No I didn't." He looked concerned as he looked at me and asked, "Do you know where they are now? Are they safe?"

I weighed my answer to him and said, "Penny is being taken care of in a safe place and nobody can hurt Lilly anymore."

"She's dead isn't she," he asked

"What make you ask that," I remarked.

"Well, first of all," he stated, "you said her daughter is safe, then you showed me a computerized picture of Lilly and a real picture of her daughter and you say nobody can hurt Lilly again. The only way that can happen is if she's dead or what ever trouble she was in was settle and obviously it's not if you are hear asking me these questions. She said if she was ever caught she believed she would wind up dead."

"Well, I'd appreciate it if it didn't go any farther than you and I, but yes she is dead," I replied.

His cheekbones tightened in his face and I notice a look of anger, yet a hint of sadness in his eyes,

"She was killed in a car accident though, not caused by anything but high speed," I explained quickly.

"So why are you asking about her?" He asked.

"I'm trying to find out about her and Penny's past." I answered. "I think I know why Lilly was on the run, but I need to know the whole story before I can help Penny and know who to contact in her family that might take care of her."

"What do you know?" he asked.

"I'd rather not say right now, but I'd appreciate any help you could give me."

"I wish I could, but that's about all I know. Lilly seemed nervous and desperate, so I helped her out, that's all there is to it," he replied. I could tell he had taken a very strong liking to Lilly, but he wasn't about to admit it.

"You said that you met her in Fargo?" I wanted to make sure I understood all the facts.

"Yes, she said she was checking out truck stops for jobs."

I shook his hand and thanked him, then I asked, "Did she happen to mention anything about U.S. Marshals looking for her?"

"Just that she couldn't trust the police for help and that she was in danger." The sincerity in this man's eyes made a lump start to form in my throat. Very seldom in my life have I met a man that looked so powerful yet so genuinely kind at the same time. I could have reached out and hugged him without a second thought, but needless to say that wouldn't have been appropriate.

"That's what Patty told me too," I commented, clearly the lump from my throat.

"I didn't catch your name," he said.

"Ricky," I replied.

He took a piece of paper out of his pocket notebook and started writing. Then he handed the paper to me. My name's Dickson. Call me at this number in a day or two. I'll see what I can find out from the other truckers."

I nodded then said, "Be discreet, I don't want anyone to know that Lilly's dead just yet. I have to protect Penny. She could still be in danger."

"I hope some day you can tell me about her. I'd like to know what had Lilly so scared too." He was genuinely concerned.

"You're an okay guy Dickson," I said, then I started to leave and turned back toward him. "I'll tell you this much, because I believe I can trust you, I think Lilly was trying to protect her daughter."

Dickson nodded his head, "That would make sense to me, thank you. Call me soon."

I nodded my head and replied, "I will." Then I left for my car.

Chapter Nine

The next stop was the library in a small down up the road, where I looked up U.S. Marshals. What I found confused me even more.

"The mission of the United States Marshals Service is to protect the Federal courts and ensure the effective operation of the judicial system." Today, the Marshals Service provides protection for the federal judiciary, transports federal prisoners, protects endangered federal witnesses and manages assets seized from criminal enterprises. Also they pursue and arrest federal fugitives.

I had to wander even more what the U.S. Marshal's office wanted with Penny. I was pretty sure that Lilly was on the run because of whoever was molesting Penny. I didn't believe that she was a federal criminal, I didn't know why. If she were a federal witness, then she wouldn't be afraid of the police . . . or would she? I would just store this information along with the rest and hope the pieces fell together eventually, meanwhile I would go to Fargo and see what I could find out. I hoped my instincts were right about Dickson and that I didn't tell him too much.

I left the library, got in my car and headed back north on interstate 94. If Lilly had been in Fargo she would have taken 94. I was glad that I had found Dickson, because now I knew which way to go next. When I got close to Fargo, I started checking out all of the truck stops along the interstate, but didn't have much luck.

Dickson had said that Lilly was stopping at truck stops to find jobs. Besides the stolen car and stolen license plate reports I had nothing else to go on, other than she didn't trust the police. I knew that it would take a lot of time, but I kept stopping at every truck stop I could find along the interstate.

Because of the lack of solid sleep the night before and the frequent stops I didn't make it very far past Fargo that day and by early evening I pulled into a small roadside inn a ways off from the freeway. I had to get a good night sleep, if I was going to keep my wits about me.

The inn was set up with quaint little cottages. Just past the desk was a small coffee shop. I went in and sat down. When the waitress came to the table I ordered a bite to eat. She smiled and walked away. Before long I found myself looking around the coffee shop at some of the paintings on the wall. One in particular caught my eye. It was a picture of a little girl with a dress and a sunbonnet on. She had a handful of daisies and was in the middle of a field spinning around in circles. There was a man standing on the top of a hill, looking down at her clapping his hands. They both had a big smile on there face. I wondered what it must be like to live like that. I had never experienced anything like that as a little girl and I was pretty sure Penny hadn't either. "Oh Ricky stop being so cynical. You can't compare yourself and Penny to the rest of the world," I mentally scolded myself.

Just then the waitress brought my order. "It's a pretty picture, isn't it," she said as she placed my order in front of me.

I nodded and sat up a little straighter, as I cleared my throat, "Oh, yes it is," I replied.

She smiled a said, "It was done by an old lady here in town. She's quite an artist."

"I'd say so," I replied politely. I thought to myself that this woman must have beautiful childhood memories and put them on canvas. Then the cynical side of me took over, as I thought, maybe she just wished it were that way.

The waitress smiled and left the table.

After eating and paying for my meal I went to my room. The rooms had a quaint rustic look about them. There were more of the old woman's paintings on the wall. There was a polished stone fireplace in the corner and what looked like a hand hewn wooden bed. I lay across the bed for a moment. It was nothing like most motel beds. They were usually hard as boards. This bed felt as though I could sink right into it and never get out. I forced myself to get back up so I could take a shower before retiring for the night.

It was a restless night for me. The case stirred up memories that I had buried deep in my subconscious for years. Once again, I was living with my foster parents. I felt the stinging and cutting of the homemade horsewhip. I felt the paralyzing fear of looking up and seeing him coming after me with a rifle. I saw myself stumbling off into the woods dodging trees and tripping over the underbrush to get away and praying he wouldn't catch me and kill me, yet almost hoping he would and put me out of my misery. I felt the pulling of my hair, the kicks to the ribs, the feeling of hands around my throat, the choking feeling and even the blows to the head and face. I remembered the anger and hurt when nobody would believe me, and the beatings, once again, when they found out I had tried to tell. I heard them warning me that if I tried to run away they'd track me down and kill me. Most of all I remembered feeling so alone and wondering if anybody really cared what happened to me or if I could just die and nobody would care that I ever existed.

That night I relived it all and woke up in a cold sweat, more determined than ever that Penny wouldn't live another day in fear if I could help it. This adult was listening and did care.

I got up and took a shower to try and wash away the thoughts that had run through my mind all night. I couldn't let my past stand in the way of Penny's future. I had to get it together and think clearly. I stood in the shower letting the water run over me until it turned cold. Shivering I got out and dried off. After getting dressed I stood and stared in the mirror for a while and gave myself a good talking to. I ate a good breakfast at the coffee shop and headed out again.

FEDERAL OFFENSE

I had just checked out another truck stop around Beach, North Dakota and was about to get into my car when a hard object was thrust into the small of my back, and a stern male voice said, "give me the keys." I was sure by the feel that the object was a handgun. I wasn't about to test out my theory by doing something stupid, so I did as I was told. "Now get in and slide over." Again I obeyed. Then the man tossed the keys to a second man that was with him and said, "Here stupid, you drive." The first man, who was short and stocky, got in the back seat, never taking his eyes off from me and still pointing the gun at me.

The second man got in and started the car without saying a word, but I could tell he wasn't too happy with being called stupid. He was slightly taller than the bossy one and very slender built.

They drove out of town and stopped at an isolated spot on the side of the road. The bossy guy got out of the car and opened my door, still pointing the gun at me. "Get out," he demanded. Then he called to the driver, "Hey stupid, get over here." The slender guy obeyed. Bossy continued, "Give me the keys, then tie her up and gag her."

"What's this all about," I asked.

Before I knew it the bossy guy hit me square on the left cheek with the butt of the gun and shouted, "shut up and do as your told."

I stumbled backward and grabbed my cheek and closed my eyes from the pain. The blow had drawn blood. I felt someone grab me and slam me down across the hood of the car. I opened my eyes as bossy said, "give me the rope stupid and yanked it out of the slender guy's hands. He grabbed my wrists and yanked then around in back of me and lashed them together. Then he forced something cloth into my mouth and tied the gag on. Pulling me to the back of the car he opened up the trunk crammed me into it and slammed it shot. Moments later the car started up again and started moving. After a few minutes I felt the car make a sharp right and the road got bumpier. I figured that we must be on a dirt road.

It wasn't long before the exhaust that was seeping into the trunk started burning my eyes, then my lungs. I could barely breath as it was, because I was fighting to keep from choking on the cloth that was crammed in my mouth and held there from the gag. The fumes were just making matters worse. I wasn't sure how long I could live under these conditions, but one thing was for sure, I was in deep trouble. Soon my thoughts were getting jumbled and everything became a blur.

I must have passed out from the fumes, because the next thing I remember was being on my knees on the ground vomiting and gasping for air. The gag had been removed, but my hands were still tied behind my back. The slender guy was saying, "Now who's stupid? You damn near killed her and the big man would have loved that."

Bossy interrupted and said, "Just shut up and let's get her into the cabin." He grabbed onto my arm and yanked me stumbling to my feet. "Let's go," He said as he pulled me toward the cabin.

Chapter Ten

Once inside the cabin the bossy one pushed me toward a couch and said, "Now you're going to tell us where that kid is." I landed so hard that the couch slid back a bit from the force. My head was pounding and my throat and eyes were burning. Needless to say I was scared. What had I gotten myself into? Who where these guys and what did they want with Penny?

I couldn't let on how scared I was, because that would show weakness and could be used against me. I sat up straight on the couch and answered through gritted teeth. "No, I'm not." I had two reasons not to tell. First of all I promised to keep Penny safe and second, my kids were there. I'd let them kill me before I'd let anything happen to those two. Annie and Jesse were my whole life and if anything where to happen to them, I might as well be dead. If I had had any brains at all I never would have let them get involved.

I guess Bossy must not have liked my answer, because he whacked me with the butt of the gun again and I could feel the blood running down the side of my face and a burning feeling in my cheek. "Look lady, I don't have time for heroics! Your going to tell me where the kid is or I'm going to have to mess you up bad."

The slender guy spoke up. "Lady, he's not kidding. If you don't want to get hurt you'll tell him."

I glared at them and replied, "You can go straight to hell." I was in deep trouble and I knew it, but I couldn't give in, not with Jesse and Annie involved.

The bossy guy prepared to strike another blow, but the slender one grabbed the gun from his hand and said, "This isn't getting us anywhere, Lou."

I was trying to study them in case I got away and could give their descriptions to Ned. Lou was the chubby one about five eight or nine. His hair use to be black, but at this point in his life it was thinning and more salt and pepper colored. He shot his partner an angry look, "That was smart Angel, why don't you just hand her our mug shots and let her go while you're at it."

Angel had to be almost six feet tall and couldn't have weighed more than a hundred and fifty pounds. His cheeks were a bit sunken and his eyes were bloodshot. He did seem a little calmer than Lou. A this point he flared right back at Lou, "Why don't you, stupid."

If I hadn't had been in so much danger I probably would have busted up laughing to hear these two idiots go at each other. I would just store those names in the back of my mind and bide my time.

Lou grabbed hold of me one more time, by the hair of my head and pulled me off from the couch and onto the floor. "Now your going to talk or I'm going to put a hurting to you, lady."

My mind flashed back to my childhood again and I thought, *he thinks he's doing something new, dragging me by my hair. He has no idea who he's dealing with. I've been brutalized by the best of them. With Annie and Jesse's lives at stake there isn't a thing he can do to me to make me talk.* I gritted my teeth once more and prepared for the worst as I replied, "Go for it blubber butt. I'm not saying another word."

Just then Lou snapped and kicked me in the stomach and ribs several times. I doubled up as I felt a familiar pain in my side, but said nothing. He sat me up on the floor and said again, "where's the girl?"

I just glared at him without saying a word. Lou doubled up his fist and punched me in the face, but I said nothing. The punching and kicking went on for quite some time, but I held my tongue, which just seemed to make him angrier. I felt like a child again, not being able to say anything to make the beating stop. In this case I had the answers, but the price I'd pay for answering would be a whole lot worse than any beating.

Finally Angel stepped in and said, "that's enough Lou. She's not going to talk."

Lou just glared at him and stomped out the door.

Angel picked me up and sat me back on the couch. "Lady, he'd just as soon kill you as not. He's got nothing to lose." Angel sounded almost as though he felt sorry for me.

"Neither do I," I answered as I spit out a mouthful of blood.

"Then this is going to be a long night." Angel stood up, shook his head as he let out a deep sigh and stepped outside with Lou shutting the door behind him.

I lay there wandering what Lou would try next to get me to talk. Then I set my mind to the task of trying to untie the rope. Actually it was bailing twine not rope. Bailing twine tangled easier when a person tries to untie it, because of all of the fine strands. It was frustrating, yet I couldn't believe that Angel had shot the door and left me alone like that. It would give me time to work at freeing myself. I worked frantically at the twine, glancing every once in a while toward the door and listening for any sign that they were returning.

I felt a catch in my ribs every time I moved wrong. I knew that feeling well from many years ago. My ribs were broken or at least cracked, but I had to try to get free while I could.

Just then I heard footsteps headed back toward the cabin door and the door opened. Lou stood in the doorway for a moment just staring at me. He walked over to the couch, grabbed hold of me one more time and dragged me into the bedroom. He pushed me down onto the bed and retied my hands, this time to the head rail. Then he wrapped the twine with electrical tape. Grabbed my legs, pulled me hard toward the foot of the bed and tied my legs together to the rail at the foot and said, "Yell all you want lady. Nobodies going to hear you. We'll be back in a day or two. If you haven't died from the heat or thirst, maybe you'll be ready to talk by then. Nobody will ever think to look for you here, so you'll either die or talk. It's up to you."

"Then I guess I'll die," I said, looking him straight in the eyes. "You might as well just get it over with."

He just stared back and said, "That would be to easy." Then he backhanded me and said, "You'll talk."

Shortly after he left the room I heard the car start up and pull away. Lou had drawn the twine up so tight that I had to work my fingertips around to feel the end of the tape. Little by little I worked at it but made no major progress. The twine was cutting into my wrists and ankles and the heat in the cabin was making me sweat, which caused all of the open wounds on my body to sting. Every time I'd try to struggle a sharp pain ran through my abdomen. My throat was dry and still burning and I was physically exhausted. I struggled to free myself until my wrists were rubbed raw from the twine. I relaxed myself for a while and closed my eyes to try to think rationally. I guess I was exhausted because even though I was in a terrible situation, I most have fallen asleep.

When I opened my eyes again it was daylight and I was soaking wet from sweat and my wounds were stinging even worse than the night before. I was stiff and sore, but as soon as my head cleared I started working on the tape that was wrapped around the twine. I couldn't believe that with the mess I was in I had actually fallen asleep. I should have stayed awake and found a way to get free.

After what seemed like several hours I heard a car pull up and someone charge into the cabin. I froze. Could they be back already? I thought Lou had said that they wouldn't be back for a couple of days. I couldn't have slept that long. I started cussing myself again for falling asleep instead of getting free while I had the chance. Then I prepared myself for the worst. What would Lou have in store for me this time? Just then I looked up to see a tall handsome looking U.S. Marshal standing in the doorway of the bedroom.

I didn't know whether to be relieved or even more scared when I saw the Marshal standing there, I just closed my eyes and prayed.

Chapter Eleven

After Becky was done talking to me she hung up the phone and mutters to herself. "For god's sake Ricky, please be careful." She prepared herself and returned to the counter. She looked at Jake and said, "Okay Jake, I've straightened out that order. They'll be calling you back tomorrow to verify delivery."

Jake smiled and said, "Thanks Becky," and returned to the kitchen.

Becky turned to Ned and Marshal Hicks. "More coffee?"

Ned gave her a curious look and replied, "sure, thanks."

"Oh Ned, did I tell you that Ricky called," Becky said.

Ned stiffened, "Oh really? How's her Uncle Harry?" He acted as though he was warning Becky not to say anything in front of Marshal Hicks.

Becky smiled and said, "He's on the trail of that bear that got into his barn. Ricky says he's determined."

Ned was relieved at Becky's answer and chuckled as he replied, "That's good old Harry. He's a tenacious sucker."

Hicks just shook his head. "You folks are definitely different than any folks I've ever met."

Ned just slapped Hicks on the back and said, "You City boys just don't know how to enjoy life that's all." Then he looked at Becky and winked.

Becky chuckled and walked away.

At St. Christopher's, Jesse and Annie sat in the cafeteria talking while Penny slept. Annie went by the hospital as often as possible to check on Jesse and to make him take a break from Penny's situation. She knew her brother better than anybody and knew that once he set his mind on a project that he could get way too involved with trying to make it all right and wouldn't stop until he drove himself crazy.

Annie looked at her younger brother and said, "Jesse I have to say that I'm sure glad that you've grown up since I lived at home.

"Why," Jesse asked.

"Because," Annie replied, "you've become more mature and you wouldn't be much help to mom and Penny if you were constantly losing control like you use to."

"Believe me Annie," Jesse looked intense, "it's not easy. Every time Penny reacts in a way that shows what she's been though, I want to go after that creep and hack him into little pieces." Jesse was talking through gritted teeth. His fists were clenched so tight that his knuckles were white.

"I know Jesse," Annie replied. "Working with the special education kids I see all kinds of things. Did you know that some of those kids end up there due to abuse or neglect?"

"Ya, I know," He answered. "How do you keep from losing it all the time. I'd be up on charges if I had to see it all the time. I know if I ever got my hands on the person that hurt Penny, I wouldn't be responsible for my actions."

"That's why you are more help to mom right here. As far as how I handle it, sometimes it eats me up. I just have to concentrate on helping the kids and let the law handle the rest." Annie smiled at her brother. "It isn't easy believe me."

"I know what you mean." Jesse stared at his meal.

Annie changed the subject. "Have you heard anything from Mom?"

"No, but I'm sure she'll call as soon as she has anything to report. I just hope she finds out something soon. The suspense is killing me."

Annie nodded her agreement and said, "Maybe I'll run by the Hitching Post later and see if Mom has called Becky."

"Why Becky?" Jesse was curious why Annie would think that their mother would call Becky and not them.

"Because Butthead," she said with a grin, "she knows that Hicks will be watching us. We're with Penny." Annie had called Jesse butthead for years and when she wanted to lighten a situation she would use it.

"Jesse chuckled, "Okay Sis, you're right."

"What do you say you get back to Penny and I'll run by the Hitching Post?" Annie stood up.

Jesse agreed and stood up too, got a smile on his face and said, "Okay, Butthead reporting for duty." He popped a salute and they walked out of the cafeteria together. When they reached the elevator Annie patted her brother on the back and said, "I'll see you later, Butthead," then headed for the exit."

Jesse nodded and headed back to Penny.

By the time Annie had reached the Hitching Post, Ned and Hicks had left and Becky was wiping down the counter. There was nobody else in the place except Kyle. They both looked up when they heard Annie enter. Becky smiled and motioned her over to the counter. "I'm glad you stopped by Annie. Your mom called earlier."

Annie looked relieved, "I was hoping she had called you. Jesse's getting impatient and I have to admit I was a bit worried."

Becky said, "She's fine and said she'd call me at home tomorrow."

"Good," Annie answered. "How is she doing on the case?"

"She says to tell Jesse that Penny's mother's name might be Lilly. At least that's the name she used at the truck stop where she worked for a sort time before she moved on. Nobody remembered seeing Penny. Lilly must have kept her well hidden. The last name Lilly used was Peters."

"Lilly Peters, Okay I'll tell Jesse next time that we're away from the room." Annie nodded in understanding of the situation.

Becky continued, "Your mom says to tell you both that she's proud of you and to tell Jesse to hang in here. That he's more help here than he knows."

Annie smiled proudly, "Mom's always saying she's proud of us and I'm glad she is. I keep telling Jesse that he's more help here every time I see him, but I'll let him know that Mom thinks so too."

Kyle sat there listening to the whole conversation, "She is proud of you two you know. I can see it in her eyes every time she talks about you."

Annie nodded, "I know she is. She never lets us think other wise."

Kyle chuckled, "You know its kind of funny in a way. Your mom doesn't act like the motherly type, at least not toward other kids, but she must show a different side of herself to you and your brother, because you all seem so close. The only time I see her truly light up is when she's talking about you kids."

Annie laughed, "She always says all three of us grew up together and we taught her as much as she taught us."

Becky chimed in. "Ricky is an old softy at heart, but I wouldn't say that to her face. She's just always felt the need to put up a tough front."

Annie replied, "You know my mom pretty well don't you?"

"After eight years of pouring coffee for her almost every morning, I would hope so." Becky said.

Kyle stood up and said, "Well I had better go try to get the chief alone for a minute and relay the news. I'll see you two later."

Annie said, "Kyle wait and I'll walk out with you." Then she turned to Becky. "I'll check back with you tomorrow, to see what Mom has to say."

Becky grinned, "See you tomorrow."

Annie and Kyle left the Hitching Post together and Becky stood there and watched as they left. Then as though she was talking to someone she said, "That Ricky is one lucky woman when it comes to her kids. I hope she takes care of herself and come home to them soon."

Jake came out of the kitchen and said, "Oh Becky, Ricky is as tough as a mama bear protecting her cubs, when she has to be. She'll be just fine."

"I hope you're right Jake. I have a feeling that there is more to this case than it seems to be on the surface. I think when I get off today I'm going to stop over and check on Jesse and Penny."

Chapter Twelve

Jesse sat in the hospital room playing Uno with Penny. "Are you tired of hanging around here all day," he asked Penny.

She nodded her head, "I wish I could run and play outside like other kids do. I haven't been outside in a long time. Mommy always made me hide."

Jesse had assumed as much. It seemed from all reports that Lilly had kept Penny pretty well hidden when they were on the run. "What would you say if I said I'll talk to Dr. Jenkins and see if we can go on a little field trip tomorrow?"

Penny's face lit up. "Can we Jesse?" She was excited.

"I don't know yet. I'll see what I can do." Jesse almost wished he hadn't said anything. What if someone put a stop to it? Penny would be so disappointed.

"Go ask him, please Jesse," Penny begged. "Please."

"Okay, I'll see what I can do, but don't get too excited yet. They could say no." He was trying to prepare her, but she was having no part of it.

"Oh Jesse you can get them to say yes, I know you can." Penny was sure.

"We'll see," Jesse replied. "You just stay right there and don't get too excited."

Jesse left the room and started down the hall. Becky was on her way to the room and met up with him at the nurse's station. "Hi Jesse. I just came by to see how you're doing. Have you got a minute?"

"I'm on a mission at the moment, but if you could wait I'll be right with you. If I don't take care of this right now Penny will be broken hearted and I can't lose ground with her, not now." Jesse was intent on his quest.

Becky just smiled and said, "I'll wait."

Dr. Jenkins was at the nurse's station looking over a patience chart when Jesse stepped up to the desk and looked straight at him. He looked up and said, "Can I help you Jesse?"

"I sure hope so," Jesse replied, "Penny is getting antsy and wants to get out for a while. Do you think it would be possible to take her to the petting zoo tomorrow or something out side and fun."

"There's nothing physically stopping her. I can't do her surgery right now anyway, but I'll have to check with Marshal Hicks," Jenkins replied, "but I'll give him a call and see what I can work out."

"Its important Doc," Jesse stressed.

"I'll get right on it." Jenkins walked over to the phone and started dialing.

Jesse turned back to Becky. "Okay I'm all yours for a minute."

Becky commented, "I think that's a great idea Jesse the poor things been stashed in one hole or another for who knows how long."

"It would sure do a lot to lift her spirits, I know that," Jesse replied.

Becky took Jesse by the arm and guided him away from the desk and spoke softly. "Did Annie tell you that your mother called?"

"Yes, she stopped by on her way home," Jesse answered.

"Good, I just wanted to make sure that you knew," Becky said.

Just then Dr. Jenkins said, "Jesse you can go, but your shadow over there has to go too."

"Jesse smiled, "I sure hope he can keep up with us. We're on a mission to take in as much fun as possible in one day."

Becky said, "Good for you Jesse. Have a good time tomorrow and I'll talk to you when you get back."

"Okay," Jesse answered as he quick stepped down the hallway to Penny's room. As he stepped inside he noticed that Penny was sitting on the bed with her eyes pinched shut and her fingers crossed on both hands. Jesse had to laugh. "Okay Penny, you can stop wishing now. We can go."

Penny started bouncing up and down and giggling with excitement.

Jesse said still laughing, "Okay Penny, you need to get some sleep now, if you want to go tomorrow, so snuggle down tight and try to sleep."

Penny did what she was told, but Jesse could still see she was too excited to sleep. So he asked, "Do you want me to read to you until you go to sleep?"

Penny nodded her head excitedly, so Jesse picked up the book that they were working on and began to read.

An hour later when Dr. Jenkins came into the room Penny was sound asleep and Jesse had nodded off in the chair. Jenkins took the book out of Jesse's hands and covered him with a blanket and tiptoed out of the room.

The next morning Annie stopped by the Hitching Post on her way to the school.

Becky looked edgy as Annie walked over to the counter. "Your mom hasn't called yet. I thought sure that she would call before I left for work this morning."

Annie replied, "Maybe she was in the middle of something and she'll call later. Here's my number at home. Call me later if you hear from her, please."

Becky nodded and Annie headed for the door. Just as she reached for the handle Ned and Marshal Hicks stepped in. "Hello Annie," Ned said as he held the door open for her.

Hicks looked at Annie and said, "Hello, Annie. What do you hear from your mother?"

Annie covered well as she replied, "She's having a great time bear hunting with Uncle Harry." As she walked up the street she chuckled to herself. "Mom bear hunting, ya right."

VENEDA (SAMMI) REED

Penny was up and dressed and sitting on the edge of the bed impatiently waiting when Jesse opened his eyes. He rubbed his eye and looked around confused at first then noticed Penny ready to go. "Just hold on there young lady, you need to eat a good breakfast first. We've got a long day of fun and play ahead of us and you need to be ready for it."

Penny looked disappointed, "Okay, Jesse."

Jesse grinned, "Don't worry the petting zoo will still be there when your done eating." He had to laugh at himself. He sounded like his mother when he said that. He had to wander if all adult sounded like that when talking to their kids.

After Penny had eaten her breakfast and washed her face and brushed her teeth, they were ready to go. Jesse took her hand and they started to bounce out the door playfully. All of a sudden Penny noticed the officer at the door and stop dead in her tracks. She turned and grabbed onto Jesse's arm with all of her strength.

It was as though her feet were glued to the floor, as Jesse started to step forward. Penny wouldn't budge. Jesse stepped back into the room and closed the door. He knelt down in front of Penny and asked, "What's wrong?"

Penny just stood staring at the door.

Jesse picked her up and sat her on the edge of the bed. "Are you afraid of the officer?"

Penny just stared. Jesse pushed the nurse's call button and held Penny's hands. "Let me see what I can do about him okay?"

Penny nodded. Just then the nurse stepped into the room and Jesse asked her to stay with Penny for just a minute while he stepped outside to speak to the officer.

Chapter Thirteen

As Jesse stepped out of Penny's hospital room he saw Ned and Marshal Hicks walking toward him.

Hicks said, "I thought you were taking Penny to the petting zoo."

Jesse replied, "She's afraid of your officer here and won't come out of the room. We need to work something out here. What is it about you Marshals that scares her? Ned and Kyle don't effect her quite that badly."

Hick didn't answer that question. He just said, "We'll work something out."

"Look," Jesse said, "the petting Zoo isn't that big. Couldn't your officer just follow us there at a distance and watch from out of sight."

"I don't know." Hicks was hesitant.

Then Ned spoke up. "The kids aren't going anywhere once they are inside. There's only one gate to go either in or out. What's the harm in giving them a little space?"

After careful consideration Hicks finally agreed and the trip was on.

Jesse stepped back into the room and took Penny by the hand, "Okay Penny he's gone. Are you ready to go now?"

Penny seemed nervous, but nodded her head and Jesse and her started out of the room once more. As they stepped out the door she searched the hallway carefully then stepped out. Jesse could feel the tension easing in her grip on him. By the time they had reached the petting zoo Penny seemed much more at ease and the officer stayed out of sight. Jesse and Penny laughed and ran and played all afternoon. They stuffed their faces with hotdogs and soda and anything else Penny asked for. Penny would bust up laughing every time Jesse would imitate one of the animals. When Jesse was imitating the pony by pawing at the ground and started whinnying Penny laughed and said, "Oh Andy, you're so funny."

Jesse paused for a moment then thought it best not to act as though he noticed Penny's slip of the tongue. "I'm funny huh, Jesse said, "No, you're funny."

"No, you're funny," Penny repeated.

"Okay," Jesse returned, "I'm funny, you're Penny."

All the while that Jesse was joking with Penny he wandered who Andy was. He was obviously someone Penny felt comfortable around. Was this someone she could turn too? He hoped that Andy was out there somewhere and that his mother could find him. Andy would be the one person his mother could trust, he was sure of that.

After their long day of fun and games Penny was exhausted and fell asleep easily that night and Jesse crawled into the bed that had been brought in for him. Dr. Jenkins had decided that Jesse didn't need to be sleeping in the chair on nights that he stayed all night. Penny was in a private room anyway, so Jesse really wasn't taking anybody's space.

Another morning began and Becky arrived at work a couple of minutes late. Jake looks up anxiously, as she stepped inside the door. Becky shook her head and said, "Nothing Jake. I'm really scared. Ricky's in trouble, I just know it."

Just then Hicks and Ned arrived for their morning coffee. Ned gave Becky an anxious look and Becky just poured the coffee and said, "How are you two today." She sounded tired. Ned knew what that meant.

Hicks asked, "Is something wrong Becky?"

"Just family problems, that's all." She looked at Ned. "You know my sister, don't you Ned?"

Ned replied, "Why yes, of course I do."

"Well," I'm worried about her. She usually calls me everyday and I haven't heard from her in a couple of days."

Hicks spoke up, "I know it's none of my business, but why don't you call her?"

"I can't get hold of her." Becky paused for a moment. "She's out at seas, she calls me by ham radio operator."

Ned knew what Becky was getting at. "Just hang in there Becky don't lose faith."

Just then Jake stepped out of the Kitchen. I've called in a replacement for you today Becky. Why don't you go home and wait for your sister to call, but first," he handed Becky a covered plate, "would you run this by to the kids at the hospital. I'm sure they're tired of that food by now."

Becky nodded, "Thanks Jake." She took the plate glanced at Ned and said, "I'll see you later."

Ned nodded at Becky and she left the Hitching Post and headed for the hospital.

Hicks shook his head as Becky left. Then he turned to Ned, "Boy, she and her sister most be close."

Ned replied, "Yes they are, very close. We all think the world of her."

"It must be nice to live in a town that's like one big happy family." Hicks was impressed.

Ned nodded and said, "Oh we have our troubles here too, but most of us get along pretty well."

Becky walked slowly toward the hospital. How was she going to tell Ricky's kids that their mother hadn't called yet? Jesse would be more determined than ever to go out there. He'd be sure he could find her. She hoped Annie was at the hospital. After all, it was Saturday and she wouldn't be at the school.

FEDERAL OFFENSE

Meanwhile, Jesse was sitting in on Penny's session with the child psychiatrist. She was trying hypnosis on Penny. Penny was acting out a physical relationship with someone then started to cry.

Jesse started to rise from his chair. He wanted to go to Penny and comfort her, but the Psychiatrist put her hand out to stop him and he sat back down. He had his fists clenched so tight that his knuckles where white, but he stayed seated.

The Psychiatrist asked, "what's wrong Penny?"

"I didn't do it right. I'm trying but it hurts. I'm sorry. I'll do it better next time," Penny sobbed.

Jesse felt a burning inside, but forced himself to sit still.

The Doctor asked, "How do you know that you didn't do it right?

Penny explained through her sobs as she puts her hand to her cheek as though she had just been slapped, "because he's is angry with me and says I'm week like mama was."

"Who is angry with you," the doctor asked.

"He is," Penny replied.

"Who is he," asked the doctor.

Penny broke down totally at this point and through her bawling Jesse heard her say, "Grandpa."

Annie was walking toward Penny's hospital room just as Jesse stormed out of the room with a look of rage on his face. He doubled up his fist and hit the opposite wall a couple of steps away from the door. The officer jumped then grabbed hold of him.

Annie ran up to them and said in a panicky voice, "Let him go, I can handle him." The Marshal stepped back quickly and Annie stepped between them. "Jesse," she yelled. "Look at me."

Jesse stopped in mid-swing. He stared at his sister then stumped off down the hall. Annie ran after him calling his name. Finally he stopped at elevator and once they step inside and the door shot, he turned and looked at his sister. He had a wild look in his eyes, as he declared, "It's her grandfather, her own grandfather, Annie. How can that be? How can a grandfather do that to their own grandchild?"

Annie hugged onto her brother. "I know Jesse it doesn't seem right."

Once they got outside of the hospital, Annie sat Jesse down and they talked the whole thing out for quite a while. Just as Jesse was settled down they noticed Becky coming up the walkway, with a covered plate in her hand.

Becky noticed their mood and asked, "What's wrong?"

Jesse had a helpless look on his face as he said, "It's Penny's grandfather who molested her. You've got to tell Mom."

Becky hesitated, "Her grandfather? Oh my God. That's sick." She sat down next to Annie and Jesse and pondered the idea for a moment then she said, "Annie can we talk for just a moment?"

Annie assured herself that Jesse was calm enough to leave alone for a minute then nodded to Becky. Becky handed the covered dish to Jesse and then she and Annie stepped inside the hospital to talk.

Becky took Annie by the hands, "I hate to do this to you right now, with all that's going on, but I'm worried about your mom. She hasn't called yet."

Annie was stunned, "Mom?" She paused then looked Becky in the eyes, "What do we do?"

"Trust in Ned," Becky replied. "He'll know what to do. He's not about to let anything happen to your mother. He cares a lot about her too you know. We all do."

"I can't tell Jesse, not right now," Annie said. "He'll really lose it and be determined to go take care of this himself and I'm not sure I could stop him."

"Let pray we hear something soon," Becky said.

Annie replied, "I've got to call my husband, but first I need to get back to Jesse. Keep me up to date okay."

Becky answered, "I will."

Chapter Fourteen

I still wasn't sure how the U.S. Marshals tied into all of this mess with Penny, so I didn't know what to think when I looked up and saw the Marshal standing in the doorway. He stood about six foot one or two and was very muscular. He seemed to be about my age. He smiled and said, "I presume that you are Ricky Rogers."

I glared at him and said, "That's me."

"I'm so glad that I found you in time. We picked up two escape prisoners in town and they happened to be driving your car. After much persuasion one of them told us about you being held here." He walked over to the bed and cut the twine and unraveled the tape. Are you hurt anywhere?" He seemed genuinely concerned for my health.

As soon as my hands were free I started rubbing them and trying to move them, to get the circulation back. I gritted my teeth from the pain in my abdomen as I sat up to rub some circulation back into my feet. As I did so I let out a groan and answered, "Mostly my pride. It's nothing I can't deal with."

He cringed as he looked at my face, as though he felt it and said. "That's got to hurt. Just sit right there for a moment and get your bearings, I'll be right back." He left the room and came back with a first-aide kit and a warm, wet cloth. As he proceeded to wash the blood off from my face, he asked, "How did you get into this mess?"

I cringed as the wet cloth touched my face and I answered, "I guess I was in the wrong place at the right time."

He jerked his hand back when I cringed and said, "I'm sorry, but this looks pretty bad. I think you're going to need stitches. Now let me see the rest of your injuries."

I was holding my ribs from the pain, but I wasn't about to lift my shirt for this guy so I pulled away and said, "I'm just fine."

He smiled and answered, "When Angel spilled his guts to us he said that Lewis did a number on you. I just want to check it out."

"It's just fine," I demanded.

"Okay. Mrs. Rogers, but I am taking you to the local hospital for an examination." He was adamant about it.

"Alright, I'll go and the name is Ricky, just Ricky." I wondered why he hadn't cornered me about why I wasn't at my uncle's place as I had told Hicks. "Do you know a Marshal Hicks?"

He stiffened at the mention of the name. "What about him?"

"Oh I just ran into him a few days ago," I replied nonchalantly, "and you don't act anything like him, that's all."

"Hicks is a maverick. You'd be wise to steer clear of him." I could tell that he didn't care the least bit for Hicks, which made him all right in my book.

"Do I just call you Marshal," I asked.

"My name is Grant, Lee Grant."

"So, Marshal Grant, who are these two goons that grabbed me?"

"Don't you worry about them, they won't be bothering anybody, for a very long time." He offered me his hand for assistance and said, "Your apt to be a little off balance, so hold on to me and I'll help you to the car and take you to the hospital. Can you stand?" This Marshal was a whole lot nicer than Hicks was. I wanted to ask more about Hicks, but I still wasn't sure how much I should let on to him. After all they did both work for the same outfit, whether they liked each other or not.

"Yes, I think so." I let out another groan as I started to get to my feet and he put his arm around my waist to help me the rest of the way to my feet and we walked carefully to the car.

The hospital put strips of tape on the gash on my cheek, because it had been to long since the injury to sew it up. They said I might have a pretty nasty scare from it. Lou had managed to crack three ribs and fracture my left arm. I had a mild concussion and was bruised up pretty good, but I'd live. They admitted me overnight. I was dehydrated and they were afraid of infection setting in on my cheek.

Marshal Grant said his good-byes once he was sure that I was alright and said he'd be by the next day to check on me and he'd bring a local officer by to take a report on the incident."

After everything settled down I called Becky at home. It was late and going on three days since my last call and I had promised to call the next day. As the phone rang I wondered how I was going to tell her what had happened. I'd have to tell her something to explain why I hadn't called in so long.

Just then Becky answered. "Hello."

"Hi Becky."

"Ricky, where have you been? Are you alright? We've been worried sick about you." I sensed the anxiety in her voice.

"I'm fine, I just ran into some complications and couldn't get to a phone." I answered.

"What kind of complications," she asked.

"Just then a nurse came into the room and said, "Excuse me Mrs. Rodgers but the doctor has ordered a shot for you for the pain."

I tried to motion to her not to say anything, but Becky had already heard. "Doctor? . . . A shot for the pain? . . . Ricky what happened to you?"

"Oh a couple of guys roughed me up a bit, trying to get me to tell where Penny was. Believe me it sounds worse then it really is. They're just keeping me over night for observation. I'll be out tomorrow and back on the road. Ow!" The nurse stabbed me with the needle.

"Is that why you didn't call?" There was tension in Becky's voice.

"Well, you might say I was tied up for a while."

"Ricky this thing is getting out of hand. You signed on to find Penny's family and who molested her, not to get beat up and tied up. Maybe you should let the police handle it from here." Becky replied.

"I can't, because I don't know who to trust besides me, Kyle and Ned." I informed her. "Don't worry. The guys that roughed me up are in jail, beside I might just have help on this end now. Have you got anymore information from Jesse?"

"Yes, but first tell me, what help?" Becky wasn't about to drop the subject.

"I'll let you know as soon as I know for sure," I answered. "What did you get from Jesse?"

"Oh, you're not going to believe this." She said. "It was Penny's grandfather that molested her."

My heart went up in my throat, as I said, "I had a feeling that it was someone in the family, it usually is they say. My god, the grandfather! Which one, does he know?"

"No, he just said that it was her grandfather. He was pretty worked up at the time. Ricky we didn't tell him that you were missing, because he was so worked up, but Annie's worried sick."

"Oh my poor kids. I've put them through hell. I never should have dragged any of you into this. Becky I need you to have Ned pull the kids out of there. If these guys could have gotten me to talk the kids could have been in real danger."

"Oh Rick I wish you could come home. This is starting to sound worse by the minute and I know Jesse won't stand for anyone else staying with Penny. She has really bonded to him. Oh, I almost forgot. Jesse says that there is an Andy that Penny bonded with. She slipped and called Jesse, Andy. I think he maybe the one to get the answers from."

"Andy, finally a name I can trust. Thanks Becky," I replied. "I still want the kids out of there, but you're right, Jesse would fight it and there is no talking him out of something he's determined to do. Well I guess I had better get off the phone. Tell Annie I'm sorry I worried her, warn the kids of my fears and tell them that I love them."

"I will, and for god's sake be careful. You're going to make me gray before my time."

"I will," I promised.

"Call me tomorrow. If I don't hear from you I'm sounding the alarm to anybody who will listen." She meant what she said and I knew it.

"I'll call as soon as I'm released just to let you know," I agreed.

"Good-bye Ricky."

"Good-bye Becky."

The shot started taking affect shortly and I started getting drowsy. Then I felt a sharp pain in my stomach and I heard my foster mother's voice, "Ricky, stop playing around and get that garden weeded." I was lying on the ground holding my stomach as she kicked me again. "Your so lazy, Ricky. Now get up and get back to work. I struggled back to my knees and started pulling weeds, but every tug on those weeds hurt my ribs so bad that it took my breath away. Soon I passed out and I heard my foster mother's voice saying, "she got careless and the horse kick her. She's so stupid sometimes," at that I jumped and woke up in a cold sweat. Then I remembered, this wasn't the first time I'd had my ribs cracked from a beating. I was ten years old the first time and had just been placed with my foster parents for two weeks. I was trembling with fear as I told myself, "Ricky, let it go. You can't let the nightmares take over your life again."

The next day Marshal Grant stopped by just as I was being released and picking up my medication at the pharmacy. He brought the local officer just as he said he was going to do. I swore out a statement making it sound as though I had no idea why Lou had beaten me, but I thought that it might be a case of mistaken identity or just hatred for women in general. I couldn't tell anybody about Penny just yet.

After I was done with them I called and left a message on Becky's answering machine, telling her that I was on my way. Then I called the number that Dickson had given me, but I got no answer. I hung up and decided I'd try again later in the day.

Chapter Fifteen

Thanks to Marshal Grant my car was released from evidence. When I was alone I reached under the front fender and unfastened the case I had stashed up there for emergencies. I was grateful that nobody had found it. I opened the case and pulled out my thirty-eight and shoulder holster and strapped it on, then I put a jacket on over it. Feeling more secure, I got into my car and headed out once more. I wanted to get as far away from there as possible and put the whole mess behind me. Shortly after I crossed the Montana line, I stopped at the first motel that I found and checked in under an assumed name. I needed to relax and sort everything out in my head before I went any farther.

I didn't have much luck relaxing, because soon after I fell asleep, my foster parents revisited me. He grabbed me by the hair of the head and pulled me to my feet, then with one hand around my throat and squeezing enough to cut off my air he yelled, "I know your seeing that boy at school. You're nothing but a slut! He comes from a worthless family, just like you. I struggled to get away, but do to lack of air I sunk to the floor and passed out. As I started coming around I heard him say, "if you have time to whore around with that boy at school, then you have time to get your work done there. Don't ever bring any of your schoolwork home from now on. You've got enough chores here to keep you busy and you're getting jobs at night to keep you out of trouble. Maybe then you'll be too tired to whore around during the day."

The next morning I woke up sore and shaking, but once again with renewed determination to save Penny from any more pain. I headed straight for the address of the person who reported their license plates stolen. It ended up being a used car lot and the plates were stolen in the middle of the night. I was getting nowhere fast. I had tried the number that Dickson had given me several times, but still there was no answer. I decided to stop at the next truck stop that I came to and see what information I could pick up. I needed to take a more relaxing route for a while though and try to get my thoughts straight, so I took a route 200, to Great Falls. I was glad I did too, because off to my right I spotted a beautiful valley. There were tall red spires sticking straight up for what seemed like miles. I wished I'd had a camera because it was so unusual that I could never put it into words. I pulled off the road and stared at them for a while, until I felt a peaceful mood sweep over me. Finally I let out a deep sigh and got back into the car and drove on to Great Falls. Route 200 was miles and miles of ranch land with no buildings in sight. By the time I reached Great Falls I had relaxed quite a bit.

Around Butte I found a truck stop and motel. I pulled in, found a phone and called Becky. There was no new news from Westfield either. I hoped that I would find out something in Seattle or before, or I would have hit the end of the line.

I sat at the counter and ordered a meal and coffee. I listen to all of the conversations as I sat there pretending to be disinterested in anything in particular. Then I heard something that peaked my interest. At the table behind me I heard someone say. "Did you hear about The Dreamer?"

Another voice said, "Yes. I can't believe someone shot him in the head. It was like an execution, I hear. He never did have much luck with women and wouldn't you know one would get him killed."

The first voice replied, "I knew there was more to that story about him and nervous Lilly. He always said he was just trying to help her out, but rumor has it the he's been asking questions about her and that's what got him killed."

The second voice said, "He had to have been hung up on her to still be looking for her."

Suddenly a terrible feeling of horror swept over me. They had to be talking about Dickson. Had I done it again? First Patty and now Dickson, only this time someone was murdered. Somebody was very desperate to find Penny and they had power alright. No wonder Lilly was so scared.

I couldn't hold my tongue any longer, so I turned around and said, "Excuse me, but I couldn't help but over hear your conversation. This Dreamer, was his real name Dickson?"

The two drivers looked puzzled and one of them said, "My god lady, you look like you've been run over by a truck. What happened to you?"

"Never mind that," I replied, "Was his name Dickson?"

"Why yes it was. Did you know him?"

My heart sunk. I couldn't believe what I was hearing even though I was sure before I even asked. "Yes," I replied, "Well enough to know that he was a nice guy. Where did this happen?"

"At a truck in Fargo."

Right then I knew it had to have something to do with our conversation. Could it have been Lou and Angel? Was that how they knew about Penny? All that I had told Dickson was that Penny was safe and Lilly was dead. That had to be it. Should I call Marshal Grant and tell him my suspicions? How much could I trust him? He was a lot nicer than Hicks was, but sooner of later it would come out that I had ignored Hicks' order to stay away from the case. It didn't sound as though Lou and Angel were going anywhere soon. Maybe I could give it a day or so, just to see if I could find Penny's family first. Finally I said, "maybe I should move away from you boys, before something happens to you."

The first truck driver looked surprised at my statement. He was a scrawny looking guy with a couple of teeth missing in the front. He asked what I meant by that statement so I explained about Patty and Dickson. Then I told them about my adventures with Lou and Angel.

The second driver who was a mid-aged partially graying fellow that sort of reminded me of Dickson, said, "Lady, we are one big family out here on the road. Granted some of us are nicer than others, but when something like this happens we all pull together. Keep heading west to Seattle someone is bound to get hold of you along the way with information. Don't worry. We have a way of getting things done without letting something like this happen again. By the way, they call me, Comet and this hear is, the Whiz Kid."

I shook their hands and said, "I really appreciate any help I can get, but I don't want anyone else getting hurt."

"Don't worry about that, The Whiz Kid replied, "Hey, Comet can we rig this lady up with a CB?"

Comet replied, "I bet we can. I'll be right back." He left the table and went to the phone.

I asked the Whiz Kidd, "Why are you doing this with the CB?"

"We need to keep track of you and before long every trucker on the West Coast will be watching out for you and trying to find out what they can about Lilly and her kid," he replied.

Just then Comet came back to the table. "We've got a CB he said it's on its way. Now lady if you want to show me your car we'll get it hooked up for you."

"The name is Ricky," I said, "and I really appreciate all of this."

"Well Ricky," he replied, You're welcome to it, but now we have to come up with a handle for you."

I answered, "Years ago I had a CB and I had the handle of Annie Oakley."

"Annie Oakley will do just fine. Now as for Lilly we'll use Lamb when referring to her and Pony for the little girl, okay," Comet suggested.

I agreed and showed them to my car. In no time the CB was installed. Then the Whiz Kidd suggested that I looked pretty busted up and that I should get a good night sleep and showed me to a motel. He told me not to worry someone would be watching over me all night.

For the first time in days I felt safe and I slept well that night. The next morning I called Becky and reported in. She seemed tense over the situation, but relieved that I had some protection and said she'd pass on the news.

Chapter Sixteen

Annie stopped in at the Hitching Post every morning to check in with Becky. As she sat there talking with Becky that morning Ned and Hicks walked in. Ned sat next to Annie and asked, "How's life been treating you Annie?"

Annie smiled and said, "Pretty good lately, Ned and you?"

Ned replied, "can't complain. Even if I did it wouldn't do any good."

Annie chuckled, "You're probably right." Then she turned her attention to Hick. "I know that it's none of my business," she said almost sarcastically, "but I have to ask anyway. What are you doing here, besides scaring a little girl half to death with your guard outside her door and following Ned here around where ever he goes?"

Hicks shifted on the stool and seemed to be picking his words very carefully as he replied, "That's confidential."

Annie wasn't satisfied with his answer and said. "I suppose that Penny is some kind of hardened federal criminal or something."

"No of course not." Hicks seemed to be on the defensive.

"Then why are you harassing her and not going after her grandfather." Annie was irritated. "I'm sure your guard has reported in to you by now that her grandfather had been molesting her."

"I knew that," Hicks answered.

"Then why haven't you done something about it?" Annie was on the verge of yelling by this time.

Hick glared at her and replied, "That's official business and not for you to know."

Annie was hot by now. "Well here's something for you to know Marshal." She got to her feet and started toward him.

Ned jumped up and grabbed Annie by the shoulders. "Now Annie, let's not say something you'll regret later," he warned her.

Annie glared at Ned then her looks softened as she said, "You're right Ned." Then she paid her tab and said good-bye to Becky and Ned, shook her head in disgust at Hicks and left the restaurant.

After Annie had left Hicks turned to Ned, "That little girl has a hot temper."

FEDERAL OFFENSE

Ned chuckled, "She takes after her mother alright, besides she does work with children and she knows this whole thing stinks. I don't understand why we're not going after this grandfather either."

Hicks looked at Ned sternly. "Because *we* are not on this case, *I* am and *I'm* handling it *my* way."

Ned looked toward Becky and showed his distaste for the whole situation as he said to Hicks, "Yah, so I see."

Hicks continued, "The only reason I let that girl and her brother anywhere near Penny is because she trusts them. Other wise they would be out of it all together, just like their mother. She *is* out of it, right?" By this point he was irritated with the whole conversation.

Becky chimed in quickly, "You couldn't pull Ricky away from this bear hunt with her Uncle Harry for anything."

"You better hope so for her sake," Hick stated firmly.

Becky stepped back a little, caught her breath and said, "believe me, none of us want Ricky in the middle of this." She meant what she said, but also knew it was too late. I was right smack dab in the middle of it all.

Shortly after Ned and Hicks had left the Hitching Post, Kyle stopped in to get whatever message I might have passed on to Becky. "So what's new Becky," he said in a lighthearted manner.

Becky was still pretty shaken up by Hicks' statement and said, "Kyle, this case gets more complicated and dangerous every day and I don't like it. Ricky and her kids are right in the middle of it, say nothing about the fact that something has already happened to Ricky and you know she isn't about to tell us how bad it is. To top it all off she's decided to carry her gun and she has half of the truckers on the West Coast determined to protect her."

Kyle sat there and let Becky get her fears off her chest, then said, "well at least she has protection Becky. If it will put you mind at ease, I know someone who drives truck out around Seattle. You remember Dave, my best friend in high school? I'll see if he can find out how bad a shape Rick really is in, but I'm sure that if they released her from the hospital, she's just fine. Now is there anything else I need to know."

"Yes there is. One trucker has already been killed over this." Becky didn't feel the least bit better after Kyle's reassurances.

Kyle stood up quickly and said, "I'll try to get hold of Dave right now." He left the Hitching Post in a big hurry.

Chapter Seventeen

After talking to Becky I went into the bathroom to splash some water on my face. There wasn't a part of my body that didn't hurt. When I looked in the mirror, I realized why. Of course I had the gash on my cheek but there was a big bruise on the other cheek and that side of my face was swollen. I had two black eyes and a fat lip. Comet was right. I did look like a truck had hit me. The air cast on my left arm was itching to the point of annoyance. I cussed Lou as I washed my face and ran a comb through my hair. Then I got dressed and put my shoulder holster on, as I said, "no more Ms Nice detective. It's time to get serious. Then I slipped my jacket on to cover the gun and left the room.

I drove back to the truck stop restaurant for a good breakfast before heading out to Seattle. When I sat at the counter the waitress came over to me, poured my coffee and said, "What will it be this morning, Ricky. I'm to make sure that you eat well and it's already paid for.

I was taken by surprise. "How do you know me and what do you mean it's paid for?"

"Comet said to look for a woman that looks like she'd just been hit by a truck and the drivers are taking care of your expenses, even the motel bill."

I didn't know what to say, so I just ordered breakfast and thanked her.

She replied, "Hey, everybody liked The Dreamer. You just get whoever killed him and we'll all be grateful."

I nodded my head and said, "If I have my way he'll pay for more than just Dreamers murder."

The minute that I got back on the freeway I heard a voice on my CB. "Break for that Annie Oakley."

I picked up the mike and came back with, "You got her."

"Beaver Teaser here. I've got you back door all the way to Idaho." Then another voice broke in, "and Papa Smurf has the front door, so sit back in the rocking chair and enjoy the ride."

The Whiz Kid had meant it when he said they'd be looking out for me. Here I was with a trucker behind me and a trucker in front of me. I was to just drive along to Idaho while I stayed between them. I didn't have to hit every truck stop on the way, because they had that covered too. It didn't take long to reach Idaho with these guys covering me all the way. Actually the guys made me stop at a motel at Coeur d' Alene Idaho. They said it would be easier to keep an eye on me there and another set of drivers would be along soon to escort me to Seattle in the morning.

Just before I got off the freeway another trucker broke for me. "Break for that Annie Oakley.

I answered, "You got her."

"This here is The Mariner out of Seattle, a baby bear from back your way had asked me to contact you. He says to tell you that your two gunslingers are doing fine and the pony is still in the coral. He also says to tell you that the Lamb was in the same mess as the pony."

I had to think about what he was saying for a minute. The Baby Bear had to be Kyle, because Smokey Bears were cops. The two gunslingers had to be Annie and Jesse considering that I was Annie Oakley. Okay that means that Kyle asked this guy to get hold of me and the kids are fine. The pony which was Penny was still safe and the lamb which was Lilly had been molested too. Finally I answered the Mariner. "Thanks for the update."

He came back, "What's your twenty? Baby Bear says to treat you to dinner on him."

I told him where I was going to be staying and he said he was almost there. When the Mariner met me in the restaurant I was shocked. It was Dave Wiggins, Kyle's old high school buddy. I shook his hand and said, "Well Dave, what a surprise to see you."

"Oh my god Ricky, you look like hell." He said in surprise. "I mean, Kyle said you'd run into some trouble and I'd heard through the truckers grapevine as well, but I had no idea."

"Well thanks a lot Dave and I was going to say that you look as handsome as ever." I replied in a joking manner.

"You know what I mean Ricky, but it is good to see you again. What happened?"

I told him the story about Lou and Angel. Then I told him how Grant had rescued me and how the truckers had adopted me."

"I know about us adopting you Ricky. I'm your front door into Seattle," he responded. "Kyle sent me copies of the pictures of Lilly and Penny and we have them circulating among the drivers, so you should be hearing something soon."

"I really appreciate all the help." I answered.

"Dreamer was well liked," Dave's eyes looked a little misty, as he continued. "He was good people." Then he got a look of determination on his face. "Besides anybody that is sick enough to do what was done to that little girl and her mother needs to get what coming to him."

"I'm going to get this guy if it's the last thing I do," I promised.

Dave took my hand and said, "I'm to tell you not to get yourself killed and to get off the case if you're in any more danger. You know, I remember Annie from school and I'd sure hate to see her lose you."

"Me too," I said, "but I have to do this, for Penny, Lilly and Dickson. I'm in it too deep now. Besides if I don't stop this guy, he could go after Penny and my kids are with her."

Dave suddenly sat up straight in his chair and replied, "I see, Ricky. You can count on me and my friends to be behind you all the way."

"I know you are." I answered.

We sat and talked for quite a while then he said, "Well Ricky tomorrow is another day and you need some rest. Don't be afraid to take something for the pain. You're covered for the night."

I nodded my head and got up from the table. "Thanks Dave," I said. Then I left the restaurant and checked into the motel for the night. I called Becky to tell her that I had met up with Dave and she seemed relieved. Then she said, "Ricky I don't like the way Hicks is acting. I think he suspects that you are still on the case."

"Why," I asked. What makes you think so?"

"He said that I had better hope you where off the case for your sake and I don't think he meant just that you would get in trouble for not backing off."

"Did it sound more like a threat." I asked.

"Could be, Ricky. It was at the least a warning," Becky answered.

"I don't like that guy, Becky and I certainly don't like the idea of him being responsible for Penny's safety. Tell Annie to stay away from him too."

"I will," she stated.

Then I continued, "Tell Kyle to watch Hicks closely. We may have the wolf guarding the hen house, if you know what I mean."

"I'm afraid I do," Becky answered with a hint of fear in her voice.

I was feeling the tension that only a mother can feel when she thinks that her kids could be in danger. "I've got to find some answers soon."

"Ricky, I know your getting desperate, but don't get careless, okay."

"I won't."

Chapter Eighteen

The next morning Dave, his buddy and I headed out for Seattle. It was a pleasant drive over the pass. When we reached Seattle Dave's buddy turned off to make his deliveries and Dave had me follow him to his delivery. Then we switched over to his pickup and went to check out the address on the stolen car report. Once again we hit a dead-end. Once we were back into Dave's pickup he said, "Ricky you're staying with Janice and me tonight. Your getting a home cooked meal and sleeping in a real bed. In the morning you'll have a fresh perspective on things."

I was discouraged to say the least, as I answered Dave. "I hope so. Maybe I'm looking in the wrong direction. Maybe I should be checking out Hicks. Maybe I should get in touch with Marshal Grant and find out more about Hicks, besides the fact that he's considered a maverick."

Just then a breaker came on the CB. "Break for that Annie Oakley."

I keyed up The Mike. "You got her," I replied.

"Hey there little lady, this here is the Comet, bringing news from down south. Are you with the Mariner?"

"Hey Comet. Its Good to hear your voice. 10-4 on being with The Mariner," I replied.

"Meet me at The Mariner's home twenty."

"Dave took the Mike and replied, "We'll be there in ten minutes."

I couldn't believe my luck. Just as I thought I had hit a brick wall Comet brings me hope.

Comet was standing in the driveway, when we arrived at Dave's. "Well Ricky, you look a little better than the last time I saw you."

"Thanks Comet. What do you have for me?"

Dave stepped up and said, "Let's take it into the house."

I nodded, "You're right."

As we stepped in the door, Dave's wife met us and gave Dave a hug, then turned to me and said, "You must be Ricky," and offered me her hand.

I shook her hand and said, "You must be Janice. Thank you so much for having me here."

"You're welcome," she said graciously. "Come on in and have a seat. Can I get you anything, coffee, tea, or pop."

"Coffee would be nice thank you," I replied.

We walked into the kitchen and sat at the table. Janice poured us all some coffee and joined us. "You know Dreamer was one of the first guys Dave met out here. He helped us get settled and recommended Dave for his job. He was a sweet guy."

"He seemed to be a compassionate person, when I met him," I commented.

"Yes he was," Janice replied. "I can't believe anybody would want to hurt him that knew him." Janice had a sad smile on her face as she thought of Dickson. "I hope you get the monster that did this."

"I'm certainly going to try," I replied. The more I heard about Dickson the more I regretted ever getting him involved. Finally I turned to Comet and said, "Speaking of that, what have you got for me?"

"Well," he replied, "A buddy of mine says that he picked up a lady and a kid in Eugene Oregon. It was definitely Lilly and Penny. Of course the lady didn't use the name Lilly, but it was her. He remembered that she didn't let the little girl talk very much."

"What was the name that she used," I asked.

"Daisy Jeffreys," Comet answered. Then he shock his head and grinned. "This lady had a thing for flowers I guess, first Lilly and now Daisy. Anyway she told my buddy that she was on her way to Seattle to find work and her car had broken down."

"Well I guess tomorrow I head for Eugene," I said, feeling as though I had gotten a new lease on life.

Janice spoke up and said, "But tonight you are going to relax. How would you like a nice soak in a hot tub? I'll bet that would feel pretty good right now."

I smiled, "A hot tub! Wow Dave you've certainly done well for yourself. I must be in the wrong business."

Dave grinned, "Enjoy it Ricky you've earned it."

Janice was a very nice young lady. She showed me to the hot tub and even gave me an ice pack for my face. She sat there and talked to me while I soaked. "Dave says that you're a tough woman and I guess he must be right. I think after a beating like you got I would have run as far away from this case as I could get."

"Do you have kids Janice," I asked.

"Dave and I have a little girl, she's the apple of her Daddy's eye. She's spending a couple of days with my folk right now," Janice said with a proud smile on her face.

"What would you do if it was a choice between a beating like this of your little girls safety?"

Janice got a serious look of understanding on her face. "You've got a kid involved in this."

"Both of my kids are right in the middle of this," I replied.

Janice stood up and walked over to the bar and poured a root beer then said, "I wouldn't want to be in your shoes Ricky." Then she gave a sigh and said, "Diner will be ready in a little while. You just relax there and enjoy the tub." Then she left the room.

At diner that night Dave said, "Ricky, Comet and I have hauls to LA, with several stops along the way so we're your escorts to Eugene. We'll be getting started about six in the morning. Is that alright with you?"

"That's just fine with me," I answered. "Now could I use your phone? I need to check in or Becky will send the posse out after me. I have a calling card."

Dave looked at the clock and said, "Forget about the calling card, I'm suppose to call Kyle at the Hitching Post in ten minutes, anyway, so you can talk to Becky then. Meanwhile Janice will show you where you'll be sleeping tonight."

. As Janice showed me to the spare bedroom and gave me a tour of the house Dave dialed the Phone. Becky and Kyle were waiting anxiously by the phone for Dave's call. When the phone rang Becky snatched it up before it had finished the first ring, "Hitching Post."

"Becky? "This is Dave how are you doing?"

"I'm a nervous wreck Dave. What did you find out?"

"Dave gave Becky the report on my condition then said, "but she's determined to get this guy and after a while you tend to forget that she's messed up. Is Kyle there?"

Becky looked horrified as she handed Kyle the phone. Dave up dated Kyle on the situation. Just as he was finishing I walked back into the room and he said, "You'd better put Becky back on the phone. Ricky wants to talk to her." Then he handed me the phone and said, "I've filled them in on the case for you."

I took the phone and said, "Becky are you there?"

"Yes Ricky I'm here," she answered.

"Just checking in to let you know that I'm still alive. Dave already filled you in on the case so the only thing I need to ask is, how are the kids?"

"Becky's voice was a little shaky as she replied, "Their fine Ricky. Doctor Jenkins is going to perform reconstructive surgery on Penny in the morning and Jesse is a mess over it, but he'll be alright."

"I wish I could be there for them," I said.

Becky replied, "Don't worry, I'll be there. I've taken the day off and so has Annie."

"What about Hicks," I asked.

"He's still asking when you're coming back. I know that he suspects what you're up to."

I could tell by Becky's voice that she was under a lot of strain, "What's the matter Becky?"

"I'm just worried Ricky."

"About what," I asked.

"Penny, the kids, you and all of us."

"I know Becky, but I hope it will all be over soon."

"I hope so," Becky stated.

"Well I had better go. I'll call as soon as I get some news or tomorrow night, whichever comes first."

"Okay Ricky. Ricky I know I've said this before but I have to say it again. Take care of yourself please."

"I will and don't worry. Good-bye Becky."

"Good-bye," she replied and hung up the phone.

The next morning we were up early and on our way to Eugene by six o'clock. I did have to admit that I felt a whole lot better after a good nights sleep and that soak in the hot tub. I knew from experience that it would take a couple of weeks for my ribs to stop hurting though.

The drive to Eugene was pretty peaceful and the three of us chatted back and forth most of the way. We pulled into the truck stop where Comet's friend said that he had picked up Penny and her mother. After Comet had mingled with the guys for a while, he came to our table and said, "I've got a hot one. Daisy and the kid got a ride in from Sacramento about a week before my buddy picked her up. She was working at a place off from I-5 north of Sacramento. Now here's a shocker for you," he said in a sarcastic manner, "She used the name Rose St. John."

I shook my head. "Another flower, that's strange. She seemed to be following I-5 North. That could lead us pretty much anywhere between here and LA. From there she could have come from anywhere, even back east again. Why do I have a feeling that I'm running around in circles." I looked at Dave. "I have to check in with Becky. Are we going on from here tonight?"

Dave asked, "Do you think you can?"

I was ready. "Let's go for it as soon as I call Becky."

We grabbed a quick bite then I called Becky. She said Penny was doing fine and would wait to hear from me in Sacramento.

About an hour down the road Dave called ahead to me. "Annie Oakley, watch your tail. There's a car coming up fast on your left. He's driving crazy, so give him room. I glanced in my rear view mirror and saw the car right on my tail. All of a sudden he veered right up beside me. That's when I saw him. It was Lou and he was pointing a gun right at me. I jerked the car as I saw him. I thought he was in jail. What was he doing here trying to kill me again? I reached for my thirty-eight. I didn't quite get it drawn when a flash came from Lou's gun.

Chapter Nineteen

The day of Penny's surgery was hard for Jesse. It was already hard enough for him to digest the fact that Penny had been molested by her grandfather, but to this extent, was beyond comprehension. He sat at Penny's bedside and held her hand. He explained that the doctor had to fix her up good as new so they were going to let her go to sleep for a while. He explained that he would be right there when she woke up.

Then the nurse started the I.V. and Penny was asleep in moments. Becky and Annie waited for Jesse in the hallway. Annie asked Becky, "Did you hear from Dave about mom's condition?"

Becky replied, "yes, I did." She was uncomfortable with giving the news to Annie, but she had a right to know.

Annie said, "Don't pull any punches with me Becky. Give it to me straight."

Becky took a deep breath and said, "Okay you asked for it." Then Becky gave her the run down and said, "But she's still going strong. Don't ask me how."

Annie shook her head, "That's my mom. When she's after someone she's not about to stop until she's satisfied.

Just then Marshal Hicks walked up to them in a big hurry. "Is she asleep yet?"

"If she isn't asleep she will be shortly. The nurse just came out from giving her the sedative." Becky replied. "Jesse is in there with her."

Hicks peaks into Penny's room and sees that Penny is asleep and says, "I need to be with her all of the time that she's asleep, Jesse so I need you to leave now."

Jesse was confused and felt a bit of rage building up inside. "Why do I have to leave? I told Penny I'd be right here when she woke up."

Hicks was in no mood to argue the point. "Look young man just do as you're told and don't give me any trouble."

Both Annie and Becky stepped into the room and stood between Jesse and Hicks. They knew Jesse's temper and was afraid for him. Annie spoke calmly but firmly to her brother, as she looked him straight in the eyes. "Jesse we don't want any trouble. We'll wait in the cafeteria until Penny wakes up. Okay?"

Jesse wasn't happy with the situation, but understood what Annie was saying. He glared at Hicks, as he turned to leave the room.

Hicks said, as they were leaving, "you can take over just as she's waking up. I promise she won't even know I was here or you were gone. By the way did she said anything as she was going to sleep?"

Jesse was still glaring at him and answered, "No she didn't." Then he left the room with Annie and Becky.

While they waited in the cafeteria for the surgery get over with, they disgusted Hicks' actions. Jesse asked," why do you suppose that Hicks did that anyway. It's not as though Penny can run away at this point."

Annie said, "It sure was odd to say the least."

Becky said thoughtfully, "You know that they use sodium pentothal to put people to sleep. Maybe he wants to be with her in case she says something."

Jesse looked up suddenly. Do you suppose he want to know what she's going to say or is he afraid of what she's going to say?"

Becky answered, "Good question Jesse."

Annie added, "Why do you suppose that Hicks never let's Penny see him?"

Becky replied, "Because Penny a deathly afraid of Marshals, more so than Ned or Kyle."

Jesse spoke up, "and why do you suppose that is?"

Annie added, "He is old enough to be Penny's grandfather."

Becky finished with, "your mother did say that it was possible that we had the wolf guarding the hen house." She thought about that for a minute, then said, "Hey your mom's the detective, not us. We're just letting are imaginations run away with us."

Jesse asked, "Are we?"

Annie replied, "It wouldn't hurt to check with Doctor Jenkins after the surgery, just to see what went on in there."

Becky answered, "alright but that's as far as we go with it. If we find out anything suspicious we leave it to your mom, Kyle and Ned, understood?"

Jesse and Annie agreed.

The surgery took forever in Jesse's eyes. He was getting more anxious by the minute. Annie did her best the reassure him that if anything was wrong they would be the first ones told. Jesse wasn't sure if he believed that but he tried to.

Finally Doctor Jenkins came over to their table and said, "She came through it like a real trouper and she should be awake shortly.

Jesse jumped to his feet and hurried back toward Penny's room and paced outside of the door, waiting for Hicks to let him back in. Becky and Annie took Doctor Jenkins to the side and Annie asked, "Doctor did anything unusual happen in there. I mean did Penny say anything and what did Hicks do?"

The doctor looked confused, "No she didn't say a word that I recall and the Marshal sat up in the observation room and watched. He did ask me to leave the speakers on, but that's all."

Becky placed her hand on the doctor's shoulder and said, "Thanks doc. We were just curious."

Doctor Jenkins gave them a strange look, nodded then left.

Becky looked at Annie, "He thinks we're insane you know."

Annie chuckled and replied, "Well aren't we."

Becky grinned, "Yes I guess we are."

Hicks finally stepped out of the room and told Jesse that Penny was starting to stir and that he could go in the room with her.

Jesse rushed into the room and sat by Penny's bed and held her hand.

When Penny opened her eyes she looked at Jesse and said, "You did stay" and smiled a tired smile.

Jesse smiled back and said, "I told you I'd be right here when you woke up didn't I?"

Just then Doctor Jenkins stepped into the room and said, "How's our little patient feeling?"

Penny gave a sleepy smile and said, "okay."

Then Doctor Jenkins got a little nervous as he said, "Now Penny in a little while you are going to hurt some and I'm going to have Jesse call me if you do. You may feel as though someone made you do something you didn't want to do and I need you to know that didn't happen. What you will be feeling is from the operation we did to make you better, okay?"

Penny started to get tears in her eyes and looked almost as though she didn't know whether to believe the doctor or not, as she answered, "Okay?"

Jesse looked at the doctor with fear in his eyes and said in a low tone of voice, "does this mean that she's going to relive it all again?"

The doctor answered, "It's very possible."

Jesse started to choke up as he asked, "when does the pain stop for her? She's so little."

Doctor Jenkins replied, "Probably not for a long time Jesse. What she has been through sometime takes a life time to get over, but she's young and we have to help her all we can and hope it's enough."

Jesse felt a burning way down in the pit of his stomach. He wanted more than anything to choke the person that caused all of this, but he also knew that even if he did it wouldn't take away any of Penny's suffering. He squeezed Penny's hand and said, "I'm here for you Penny and we'll learn to understand this together, Okay."

Penny nodded her head. She did feel better knowing Jesse was with her.

Then Jesse picked up the phone and called Becky's number. Of course Becky wasn't home yet, but he needed to leave her a message. He didn't want to leave Penny and he didn't want her to know what he had to say either, so he spoke in code to Becky's answering machine. "Becky this is Jesse. Tell Ned or Kyle that I just have to know if there is a wolf in the hen house."

After he hung up the phone Doctor Jenkins put his hand on Jesse's shoulder. "Are you going to be alright with this Jesse?"

Jesse shook his head, "No Doc, but I have to do this for her sake." He nodded in Penny's direction.

Doctor Jenkins nodded his understanding and said, "Don't be afraid to call for help. We'll have her pretty well drugged up for the next twenty-four hours, so she should relax tonight. Tomorrow could be rough. I'll be sure that her Psychiatrist is aware of the situation. I'm sure that she'll stop by tomorrow to check on her."

"Okay doc," Jesse replied.

Then Doctor Jenkins left the room and stepped out into the hallway to explain the situation to Annie and Becky. When he was done explaining he turned to Becky and said, "by the way Jesse called your place and left a strange message."

Becky was curious. "Oh what did he say?"

Something about needing to know if the wolf is in the hen house."

Becky grinned and said, "Oh, okay I'll check for him." She had a good idea what this was all about, after Doctor Jenkins' explanation of what Penny might go through. She knew that Jesse would be more determined than ever to find out if Hicks was Penny's grandfather or at least in cahoots with the grandfather. She really couldn't blame Jesse for being impatient he had to sit there day after day and watch Penny's mental suffering. It had to be hard. She had only witnessed one episode and it affected her more than she could put into words. She could only imagine how Jesse felt.

When Kyle came into the Hitching Post the next morning to get any messages for Ned, Becky updated him on the search for Penny's home then she asked, "Kyle is there any way to run a check on Hicks, without getting in trouble?"

Kyle thought for a minute then said, "I don't know. Why do you want to run a check on him anyway?"

"Just a suspicion more than anything," Becky replied.

Kyle studied her for a minutes or two then said, "I'll ask Ned, but I'm sure his not going to be happy about this. He's been ordered to stay out of it."

Becky said, "I know Kyle, but what if he was ordered by the guilty party? After all he sent Ricky out there to find out what she could anyway. She's putting her neck on the line every day for this case. Doesn't that count for something?"

"Okay! Okay! I'll talk to Ned," Kyle conceded. "I'll relay your feelings on the matter as well, I promise."

"Good," Becky said, feeling much better about the whole situation.

Kyle just shook his head at Becky and grinned, "You're a tough one Becky. Oh by the way the next time that you talk to Ricky you may want to warn her that Hicks is starting to get suspicious of her. He's not sure that he buys the story of the bear hunting trip."

Becky felt a little edgy as she stated; "I had a feeling this was coming. I'll tell her when she calls next time.

Chapter Twenty

Between the jerking motion I made when I saw Lou and flinching I did when the gun went off, I had managed to cause the car to hit the shoulder of the road and it rolled out into the brush and came to rest on it's side. I quickly grabbed the mike as I finished reaching for my gun, "Dave stay back, just call for help. I've got it covered." Then I switched off the CB, climbed out of the car as quickly as I could and took off into the brush even farther. Lou had pulled off the road by now and was working his way cautiously toward my wrecked car. As he peaked inside the car he started cussing. I said under my breath, "to bad tubby you lose again." My hand was shaking as I held the gun poised to shoot if necessary. I was an excellent shot on the ranch. I could hit all the vital places on the paper silhouettes with no problem, but that was paper. I'd never been put in a position before where I'd have to take another human life. Researching court cases was a whole different situation all together. This was a real human being armed with a gun and he would shoot me if he had the chance, after all he did just try. Knowing all of this didn't make it any easier to think of killing him. I was sure I would if I had to, but the thought didn't exactly thrill me. I stood there crouched down behind some brush hoping that I wouldn't have to shot him, yet I wanted to get him in a position where I could get some answers from him.

Lou started working his way in circles around the car, searching the brush then he said, "You might as well come out lady, I'm going to find you sooner or later. Why not make it easy on yourself?"

He was getting closer with every pass and I knew it wouldn't be long before I'd have to act. I concentrated hard on steadying my hand and preparing for the inevitable.

Just then the smell of gas hit me and I glanced toward my car. There was smoke streaming up from it and I could see moister running down. It was going to blow soon and there wasn't a thing I could do at this point to stop it. If I were lucky it would take Lou with it.

Lou was still circling. If the explosion didn't kill him it would at least shake him up. Just as I thought he was going to spot me the car blew up and I shifted positions to a spot where I felt that I could get better access to him if need be.

Lou had hit the ground when the car blew and was now back on his feet. Just as he spotted me and jerked his gun in my direction. I felt my finger tightened on the trigger, then I heard a shot and a bullet splintered the tree right next to me. I instinctively fired a shot back, hit the ground and rolled behind a rock. Lou jerked his left shoulder a bit as though I might have hit him then fired once again. A piece of the rock chipped off and struck me on the side of the face. I fired again. That shot seemed to have had a strange echo. This time Lou dropped to the ground. I didn't hit him or did I? Just then I heard Dave calling out to me. "Ricky, are you alright."

I stumbled to my feet as I answered back, "Ya, I'm fine." Just then I saw Marshal Grant holding a rifle and rushing toward where Lou had fallen. He quickly checked him out and said, "He won't be bothering you any more." He looked up at me and asked, "are you sure that you're alright."

"Ya I'm fine, but how did he get here. I thought you had him locked up. Not that I'm not happy to see you."

"He managed to break out of jail, while we were at the hospital getting your statement. I was suppose to transport him back to the federal prison the next day, but he had other ideas. I guess that jail wasn't as secure as it should have been. I've been tracking him ever since." Grant gave me a curious look then asked, "what are you doing in Oregon anyway? You sure do get around."

"I'm searching for something," I replied.

Just then Dave reached us and hugged onto me. Thank god you're alright. That scared the bageebers out of me. I sure am glad the Marshal here was right behind us."

"Me too," I replied, "I sure wasn't looking forward to having to kill him."

The marshal looked at me with a look of concern on his face as he said, "I hope you have a permit to carry that," as he pointed at my gun.

I said, "As a matter of fact I do." I pulled out my permit and my Private detectives badge and license. "I'm on a case right now, but I'd rather not discuss it with anyone at the moment."

Grant nodded, "I see and what does your case have to do with Lou here?"

"I don't know. You tell me. What were you originally taking him in for," I asked.

Grant acted as though he wasn't sure that he wanted to tell me, but finally he answered, "Lou's little brother liked to kidnap little girls, taking them to other states, raping them and eventually killing them. He was the worst of all sleazeballs. He even raped and molested other family members. It's believed that he had an accomplice, a woman in her early twenties. She'd sometimes pass the little girls off as her daughters and transport them over state lines to Lou's brother. You had the honor of meeting him too. Soft spoken Angel. Lou was always covering up Angel's messes. There's not much known about the woman as of yet."

I didn't know what to believe. Could Lilly, Daisy, Rose or what ever her name was be this woman? Was Penny Angel's next target? No, she would have had to be his last target, but could he convince her that he was her grandfather. Maybe he was her grandfather. Grant did say that he raped and molested his own family members. Something just didn't feel right about any of this. "Why is this the first I've heard of this. I mean I've heard of kids being taken but their bodies are usually found close by eventually."

"Not all cases make the news. There are hundreds of kids kidnapped every year and most of them don't make the news," Grant answered.

I shook my head and uttered, "and I didn't want to have to take a human life, but brother or no brother he is as guilty as Angel. If I had known I wouldn't have had any bones about shooting earlier. Of course I'd rather have Angel in my sights right now."

Grant smiles and said, "it was my responsibility to get Lou. I'm glad I was the one to take him. The paper work is less messy that way."

"Speaking of Angel did he get away too and if so where is he?"

The Marshal replied, "I'll get him too eventually. I imagine he's hiding under a rock somewhere waiting for his big brother to clean up his mess for him once again."

"Well Marshal Grant, I hope you get him. Men like that turn my stomach," I said.

Should I say anything to Grant about Penny? I wasn't comfortable enough with his story yet to reveal what I knew about Penny. I needed to know more.

Just then the fire department and medics arrived and the marshal said, "once again ma'am, let the medics check you out for any injuries."

"Honestly I'm fine other than being shook up. My seatbelt gave me a little burn but other than that I came out of this pretty lucky."

Dave chimed in, "come on Ricky it won't hurt to check it out."

"Okay, I'm going," I replied.

My old bruises were more green than black and blue by now, so it was easy to tell which were the new ones. After checking me over the medic said, "well lady it looks as though you came out of this one better than the last one. Do you make a habit of this?"

I wasn't about to explain it all again so I just replied, "Not usually, just lately."

He smiled, "You could have a few aches and pains for a few days, but I'm not sure that you'll notice the difference."

After I was checked out, a wrecker came along to pull what was left of my car out. I looked at Dave and said, "Now what?"

Grant handed me a card and said go down to the next exit, go to this address and tell them Marshal Grant sent you and they'll fix you right up with a new car. Rusty owes me a favor anyway and it was my prisoner that made you lose your car, so it works out fine.

I'll call ahead and tell Rusty you're coming." He looked at Dave, "don't worry it's not very far and it will be easy to get your rig in and back to the freeway."

"Marshal I may want to talk to you later on. Is there any way to get hold of you?" I didn't want to say anything yet, but I was curious about Marshal Hicks and soon I would want some answers about him. First I wanted to find Penny's family and find out the true story.

The Marshal gave me a card and I tucked it away in my pocket. Dave and I climbed into his truck and drove off to the place the Marshal had sent us to pick up a new car.

The marshal meant it when he said he would furnish me with a new vehicle, but it wasn't a car. It was a beautiful, brand new, burgundy and black, heavy-duty Chevy pickup, fully loaded. It had a beefed up front bumper and roll bars. Rusty said, "Marshal Grant insisted on something with roll bars. He told me that you have a tendency to attract trouble and would need this feature."

I chuckled, "I guess I have lately."

"You do know that the Marshal has taken care of all expenses, don't you," Rusty asked.

"Yes I do," I replied, "and I am very grateful to him."

After thanking Rusty and shaking his hand, Dave said, "Ricky I think we need to chuck the idea of going on tonight and get a fresh start in the morning."

I agreed and said, "Lets find a place to sit and talk all of the events of the day over. I had also better try to call Becky." I paused for a moment then continued, "she's not going to like this report."

Dave shook his head. "No I don't think she is."

Comet found a place for us to stay for the night then we found a diner and got some coffee. "Dave," I said, "You and Comet don't need to worry about me anymore and go ahead and deliver your load. Lou's dead and I don't believe that Angel is brave enough to try anything on his own."

"Are you sure about this Ricky?" Dave wasn't happy about leaving me, but he did have a load to deliver and I had already slowed him down way too much. "Alright but first we get you another CB and I'm still putting the word out to watch out for you and give you whatever information anyone has got for you."

I agreed with him, then I said, "you know, there is some things that just doesn't match up, between my case and what Grant told me. That's why I didn't tell him about Penny."

Like what" Dave asked.

"Penny's mother for example," I said. "Penny said in one of her sessions that her mother was molested too. Would someone that was molested let her father molest her daughter and if so why were they on the run?"

"Well I'm not an expert on these matter's by any means," Dave replied thoughtfully, "but I understand that many people that have been molested will act out and sometimes stay in those situations, because that's all they know. Maybe that's the case with Penny's mother. Maybe she wasn't running from Angel. Maybe she was running from the police. After all she was killed in a wreck running from Kyle wasn't she."

"You have a point there and I guess her fear of police could have rubbed off on Penny. If the U.S. Marshal's office was on their case she would be even more afraid of them." I thought about that for a moment then said, "There's still something there that isn't right and I just can't put my finger on it."

FEDERAL OFFENSE

Dave smiled and said, "Ricky, I learned a long time ago that if it doesn't feel right it probably isn't right. I'd say you should go with your gut feelings."

I nodded in agreement and said, "Me too." Then I looked at the clock and said, "Well I had better call Becky."

Dave stood up and said, "I'll go track you down another CB."

I went to the pay phone and dialed up Becky's number. "Hello Becky."

"Ricky, I wasn't expecting you so soon. You can't be in Sacramento already."

"No I'm not," I answered. "We ran into a little trouble, but everyone is alright."

I could sense the tension in Becky's voice as she asked, "what happened this time."

I told her the whole story of how Lou had taken a couple of pot shots at me, how my car blew up and how Marshal Grant had shot Lou.

Becky didn't say anything for a few moments then stated; "I don't like any of this Ricky. You're going to end up getting killed and Penny's still going to be hurting. I wish I knew a way out of this for all of us, but I don't. Ricky there's more."

"Like what," I asked.

She told me about Hicks' actions the day of the surgery and that Penny was having a hard time dealing with the after effects. Then she said, "the kids and I think Hicks' is either Penny's grandfather or he knows the grandfather, but where does this Angel character fit into this or does he?"

"I'm not sure if he does, but I don't like what's going on back there. I think we had better find a way to get Penny out of there and away from Hicks until we know for sure what he has to do with any of this. Did you tell Ned about any of this," I asked.

"I told Kyle and I told him that Ned needed to check into Hicks whether he was scared or not."

"Good," I replied. "I know we're putting Ned on the spot, but we need to make sure that Penny and the kids are safe."

"I know Ricky, but I'm worried about you too. Someone wants you out of the picture and I'm afraid it's not over yet, what about Angel? He could come after you next or get someone to."

"I don't think Angel has the guts to come after me himself and Lou has always protected him from the violent end of things. Lou is dead and I think Angel will be too busy running from Marshal Grant to worry about me," I answered.

"I sure hope you're right Ricky" Becky commented. "I'll try to set something up with Ned and Kyle to get Penny out of the hospital as soon as possible and possibly even get her away from Hicks. This could be a tricky one."

"Becky don't get yourself into trouble," I told her.

"Don't worry about me, you just take care of yourself. I'll let Ned handle this end," she answered.

"I hope I get some information in Sacramento that can clear up some of this confusion," I added.

"Me too," Becky replied. "I don't know how you do it Ricky. I'm already frustrated and I'm not the one actually doing the investigating. I can only imagine how frustrated you are."

"I'm just worried about all of you back there. I have to find some answers soon, for Penny's sake and to get you and the kids out of this mess. Never again will I involve my friends and my kids in one of my cases."

"Ricky, we really didn't give you any choice. We just dove right on in there with you, so don't blame yourself. Just get this guy and come home safe okay."

"I'm certainly going to give it my best shot," I answered. "Give the kids a big hug for me and tell them I love them."

"You know I will Ricky and take care."

"I will. Good-bye Becky."

"Good-bye."

I didn't sleep very well that night. I kept running all the information over and over in my mind. I even tried starting at the beginning. Penny's mother seemed to be afraid of everybody especially the police. Penny had been molested, but so had her mother. Penny says it's her grandfather, but who is her grandfather. Is it Hicks or Angel or somebody else all together? Both Hicks and Angel were good possibilities. Finally I convinced myself to try to get some sleep and hope that Sacramento held the key.

When I got up the next morning Dave was waiting for me. "We have you set up with a new CB Ricky."

"Thanks Dave, now don't worry I'm just going to check out this lead in Sacramento and Lou can't hurt me."

Dave nodded then said, "The guys are out there willing to help, don't forget that."

"I won't," I replied.

I had a quick breakfast then headed out for Sacramento. The minute I got onto the interstate I was greeted by several truckers headed my way. I was in a virtual convoy all the way to Sacramento.

I had a real stroke of luck this time. I found the car that Penny's mother had arrived in Sacramento in. It was registered to a Blossom Johnson. Blossom was her real name. That's why she used the names of flowers, because it was so close to her real name. Blossom Johnson was from Beverly Hills, California. At last I knew where I was going.

I was so excited that I had to find a phone and let Becky know right away. Once I got to Beverly Hills, I hoped I would get all the answers.

Chapter Twenty-One

Jesse sat in the hospital room watching Penny sleep. He knew that soon the numbness would wear off and the nurses had reduced the dosage of her pain medicine, so he would have to be prepared for the worst. Deep inside he felt capable if doing damage to Hicks or whomever was responsible for Penny's agony and he would have no regrets. He remembered all of what he had been told through the years about everyone having goodness in them and the taking of any human life should not be an easy thing to consider. In his heart he knew this was true, but he couldn't begin to think of the person who hurt Penny as human.

As he sat there mentally torturing the guilty party, Penny began to squirm, then let out a blood-curdling scream. Then almost as quickly started crying begging for forgiveness, "I'm sorry Grandpa. I didn't mean to yell. I'm trying not to cry. Yes grandpa, I'm a baby. I'm bad. I'll do better." She curled up into the fetal position and repeated over and over again, "I'm weak like mama."

Jesse reached out and took Penny's hand into his and rubbed it gently, "I'm here Penny. Grandpa gone. It's only me, Jesse and I'm not going to let anybody hurt you."

Penny opened her tear filled eyes and cried, "Andy, tell Daddy I need him to come home, please."

Her plea broke Jesse's heart as he held her hand and said, "We're looking for Daddy now, honey. We'll bring him as soon as we find him. Okay?"

Penny nodded her head and tried her best not to cry. Then beginning to return to reality she said, Jesse's name as though she was just recognizing him then said, "I was bad wasn't I?"

Jesse felt a lump rise up into his throat as he replied, "No honey, you weren't bad at all. I know it hurts and you can't help how you feel. I would cry too if I hurt like that." As he spoke he pushed the nurses button. He continued, "It's never bad to cry when you hurt. Don't let anybody tell you that your bad if you cry."

Penny looked confused, "But he says I'm weak and weak is bad."

Jesse was having trouble speaking without chucking at this point. He cleared his throat and declared, "Penny you are very strong for such a little girl. You are not weak and I'm proud of your courage."

Penny gave a weak smile and asked, "I am?"

Jesse smiled back and said, "Oh yes Penny, very strong."

Just then the nurse arrived and asked, "How are you doing in here?"

Jesse turned to the nurse with a pleading look and asked, "Can you help her?"

The nurse looked at her watch then to Jesse with a sympathetic look, "Do you think you can help her hold on for another half hour?"

Jesse nodded hopelessly, "I'll try."

The nurse placed her hand on Jesse's shoulder and said, "I hope your mother knows what a fine young man you have become."

Jesse replied, "I use my grandfather as my example. He was a kind and gentle man from what I have heard of him and I want to be just like him." He looked at Penny then back at the nurse. "Every grandfather should be like mine, wanting the best for their grandchild," then his face changed as though he just tasted something bitter, "not this."

The nurse replied, "You're right Jesse, but unfortunately that isn't the case and poor little things like this most suffer." She rubbed Penny's head gently and said, "I'm proud of you young lady. You're doing so well."

Penny smiled shyly and replied in a soft voice, "Thank you."

After the nurse left the room Jesse squeezed Penny's hand gently and said, "See I told you that you were strong, even the nurse thinks so."

Penny was feeling better about herself at this point and changed the subject, "Jesse, do you think you can find my Daddy? He went away a long time ago and never came back."

Jesse answered, "My mom is trying very hard to find him, but why did he leave?"

"I don't know," she replied, "He just told me he was sorry, but he couldn't live up to grandpa. What does that mean?"

"I'm not sure what he meant by that, but maybe we can ask him when we find him." Jesse answered. "Penny, who's Andy?"

Penny got a big smile on her face, "Andy is my friend, but Grandpa says to stay away from him. He says Andy is a freak."

"Why does he think Andy is a freak?" Jesse was trying to keep Penny's mind occupied and still get a clear picture of who Andy might be.

He says Andy is weak like Daddy and he'll never be a real man, because Andy is an actor."

"Oh," Jesse replied, "Do you think Andy is weak because he is an actor?"

Penny shook her head. "No Andy is my friend, but I can't tell grandpa." Then tears started to show in her eyes, "Grandpa will hurt Andy if he knows."

"I see." Jesse really didn't see why being an actor was so wrong, but he was sure that Penny's grandfather had a warped way of reasoning anyway. It was obvious after what he had put his granddaughter and daughter through.

Annie stopped by the Hitching Post to check in with Becky, after checking on Penny and Jesse. As she walked in she met up with Ned and Hicks leaving. Hicks looked irritated as he greeted Annie and said, "what do you hear from your mother."

Annie, not being in the mood to talk to him just replied, "Not a thing. I guess she's busy." Then she walked right by him and smiled at Becky as she sat at the counter. "How's life Becky?"

Becky smiled back and replied, "not bad."

Hicks just glared back over his shoulder for a moment then turned and left the restaurant.

After they had walked out of sight, Becky filled Annie in on the news about Blossom being from Beverly Hills.

"The next time you talk to mom tell her that Penny wants her daddy to come get her," Annie said. "Evidently her father was driven off by the grandfather and Andy is an actor that grandpa didn't want Penny around. Penny says that grandpa would hurt Andy if he knew they were friends."

Becky shook her head, then said in a sarcastic manner, "Boy this guy is a real sweetheart."

Annie agreed, "He sure sounds like it. Jesse says from what he can gather from his and Penny's conversation that according to Grandpa Andy was week and a freak because he was an actor. Also Penny's dad was a week man too in Grandpa's eyes."

"This guy sounds more and more lovable by the minute," Becky continued her sarcastic tone."

Annie nodded her agreement then said, "Becky do you think mom will find the answers in Beverly Hills?"

Becky replied, "I sure hope so. It's time she comes home while she still had a body to come home with." Then she got a grin on her face as she continued, "well at least she got a new truck out of the deal."

"Ya, Mom's always wanted a boss looking truck." Annie got a grin on her face, "She's always been different than most moms. On Christmas, instead of perfume and flowers, she was happier with tools and practical stuff. That truck sounds like something mom would love."

Becky chuckled, "Ya your mom is a strange one. On one hand she's practical and on the other hand she does some wild and crazy things. I guess that's what makes her so interesting."

Annie got a sad smile on her face and said, "That's mom. God I wish she'd hurry home. I miss her."

Becky placed her hand on Annie's and said, "I know she misses you and Jesse too. Every time she talks to me she says to tell you two that she loves you or that she's proud of you. This isn't easy for her either you know."

Annie nodded and said, "I know and I know why she has to do this too. Did you know mom was abused as a child?"

Becky gave a knowing look and said, "She's said stuff over the years that told me she was."

"I guess mom's determined to do this for Penny because there was nobody to believe her when she was little. In fact everyone thought she was lying when she tried to tell them. Her classmates believed her. They saw her torment, but only two adults ever believed her and they weren't in a position to help much. She knows what Penny went through and she needs to put things right."

"I believe you're right Annie. Your mom is facing her demons. It just scares me to think what kind of danger she has put herself into."

"Me too," Annie replied.

Just then Kyle walked in and sat beside Annie and said in an irritated manner, "That Hicks is a pain in the butt."

Annie and Becky both turned their attention to Kyle, "Why."

"I can't do anything in that office without him standing right there." Kyle explained. "I'm trying to get some information on him, like you asked me to do, but he seems to be everywhere at once. To make matters worse he makes everyone around him feel inferior to him. It's like he believes that he knows who is superior to whom. I can't explain it but it's frustrating. You know I use to love going to work every morning, but now it's a mental argument with myself every morning to convince myself it won't last much longer."

Annie studied Kyle's face as she asked, "Would you say that he thinks of you as weak?"

Kyle looked shocked, "Yes, weak, that's it. He acts like I'm weak or simple compared to him. It's like he thinks he's god or something."

Annie looked toward Becky and nodded, "He thinks he's god huh."

Becky wanted to agree but she also didn't want to jump to conclusions so she said, "now Annie everyone feels that way at times about someone. Let's just sit back and study this situation. Your mom will probably have some answers soon and we'll know for sure who we're suppose to be on the lookout for." Then she turned her attention back to Kyle. "Have you and Ned given any more thought to getting Penny out of there as soon as she's well enough."

"Kyle nodded, "Ya, we're working on it. Ned says his uncle has a cabin out in Green Oaks that few people know about. If we have to we can hide her out there."

"How are we going to get her past Hicks and his sentry," Annie asked.

Kyle looked at Annie and said, "you aren't going to do anything. Your husband would kill us if you got hurt, to say nothing about what Ricky would do to us. It's bad enough that Jesse has to be involved, but Penny would be petrified without Jesse."

Annie replied, "Okay, Kyle how are you going to pull it off?"

Kyle answered we're still working on that. We really can't do anything right now. Penny needs the doctor right now and can't be moved."

Just then Hicks walked in and everyone suddenly got quiet. He paused for a moment and got a suspecting look on his face. Then walked over to Kyle and said, "Officer Jefferson the chief needs you."

Kyle got to his feet and said, "Yes sir," then left quickly.

Hicks looked at Becky and Annie and said, "I don't know what's going on here, but I'll get to the bottom of it sooner or later. I just hope you ladies are smart enough to know what's good for you."

Annie replied, "We know right from wrong Marshal."

Hicks wasn't sure how to take that statement as he said, "I sure hope so." Than he gave a warning look and left.

Annie looked at Becky, "Yup, he thinks he's god."

Becky cautioned : "Annie, don't forget there is someone else to consider here. This Angel character is a definite possibility as well. After all he and his brother Lou tried to kill your mom twice now."

Annie replied, "You had to remind me of that didn't you?"

Becky answered, "Sorry but it is a possibility."

Annie said, "God this is frustrating. Poor mom must be even more frustrated than we are. I'll bet there is times when she wishes she was back in the courthouse looking up paperwork."

Becky answered, "I know she'd be happier in one respect."

Annie asked, "what's that."

Becky replied, "You and Jesse would be safer. She has said several times that she wishes none of us were involved in this."

"And I bet she blames herself," Annie added.

"Becky nodded, "Yes she does, but I told her we jumped in she didn't drag us into this."

Annie replied, "Yes we did didn't we? Next time you talk to mom tell her we love her too and we're being careful."

Becky answered, "I will.

Chapter Twenty-Two

I arrived at the grapevine going into Los Angeles by evening and decided to spend the night there and check out Blossom Johnson's Beverly Hills address the next morning. After I checked into the motel I called Becky to report in. She gave me the news about Andy being an actor and that the father left because of the grandfather. She also told me about Annie's suspicions about Hicks and that Penny was having a hard time dealing with the after affects of the surgery. None of this set well with me. I hated the thought of Annie even talking to Hicks and Penny's situation haunted me more and more all the time.

That night I had more nightmares of my childhood. I remembered how helpless I felt. The next morning I woke up drained and frustrated. I had to force myself to focus on Penny's case and not relate it to my own past. All the way to Blossom Johnson's address in Beverly Hills I wondered what I would find. This was a very high classed neighborhood. Under any other circumstances Penny would be considered one of the fortunate ones. It just goes to show that wealth doesn't buy security.

The Johnson home was big enough to board a couple of families. The yard was well manicures. I could tell that a professional had kept it up.

As I pulled into the driveway an elderly man next door was returning from walking his dog. I called out to him, "Excuse me sir. Is this the address of Blossom Johnson?"

The man looked at me as though I was a gangster or something and said, "Yes it is, but she hasn't been home for quite a while."

I realized that the man had every reason to fear me. I knew I must be a frightful sight. My body looked like I had been in a gang war or something by this point. I pulled out my card and said, "I'm a private investigator, working on a case involving her daughter Penny."

The man put his dog into the house and came over to where I was standing. "Is that sweet little thing in trouble."

"Oh she hasn't done anything wrong. I'm trying to help her be reunited with her family," I replied. "You see her mother was killed in a car accident, while traveling across country and I've been trying to find her family ever since."

The old man shook his head sadly and said, "Blossom was a nice lady and Penny is a sweet little girl. This breaks my heart."

"Do you know Penny's father," I asked.

The man shook his head again. "No I'm afraid that I didn't know anybody but the two of them. They were both very quiet, but polite. You might check with Penny's school though. It's right around the corner on the left. They might know something that could help."

I held out my hand and said, "Thank you very much for all of your help."

The man shook my hand and said, "Tell the little one that I'm praying for her."

"I surely will sir and thanks again," I answered.

I got back into the truck and drove around the corner to the school.

When I had finally been lead to the office, the principle greeted me coolly, as he said, "how may I help you?"

Once again I flashed my card and said, "I'm looking for some information on Blossom and Penny Johnson. I understand that Penny went to school hear." I showed the man a picture of Penny.

"Oh yes, Miss Penelope, but I'm not at liberty to give out any information on any of our students."

"I understand," I replied, "but these are extenuating circumstances. You see Penelope and her mother were in a car wreck and only Penelope survived. I am looking for any family she might have left. Right now she is in the hospital and is asking for her Daddy. Do you have any way of contacting him."

The principle seemed unmoved by my story and answered. "I know nothing about a father. All I know about this child is that her tuition was paid by an anonymous source and I met her mother once. Penelope was very quiet and withdrawn. Then one day she just disappeared. That's all I can tell you now excuse me I have other business to attend to."

There was a young man mopping the hallway, which seemed very interested in our conversation and the principle seemed annoyed with him for not moving along. He spoke sharply to the young man. "Mr. Collins have you run out of things to do today?"

The young man started mopping faster as he replied, "No sir. I'm sorry sir."

I stalled for a while until the principle moved on. I wrote down the number to my motel room on the back of my card and as I left the office I slid the card to the young man and said in a low voice, "call me later."

He nodded discreetly then went about his business. I didn't know why but I had a feeling that this young man knew Penny better than anyone else at that school. He sure seemed interested in what I had to say and I didn't believe that he was just being nosy. After I left the school I asked around the neighborhood and nobody seemed to know much about Penny and Blossom, other than they stayed to themselves and were very quiet.

By the end of the day I was terribly discouraged, so I went back to the motel and checked in with Becky and waited to see if the young man would call.

As I waited I ordered some dinner to eat in my room, so I wouldn't miss his call, *if* he called. Later that evening, while I was sorting through my notes trying to make sense of the facts the phone finally rang. I answered it quickly, "Hello."

The voice on the other end stammered a bit as he said, "Is this the lady that was at the school earlier today?"

"Yes it is," I answered, "Is this the young man in the hallway?"

"Yes ma'am. Is Penny safe?"

"Yes for the moment," I answered. "Can I meet you somewhere?"

There was a hesitation then he asked. "Where are you right now?"

I told him what motel I was at and he said, "I know where that is I'll meet you in one hour in the lobby."

"One hour it is," I replied. "Thank you for calling."

"Yes ma'am. I'll see you in one hour. Good-bye," he replied.

"Good-bye," I answered.

The hour seemed to take an entire week to pass. I had a gut feeling about this young man. I just knew that he was the answer to my problem. I don't know why I thought so, but I did.

Finally the moment arrived. The young man walked into the lobby and I stood up. When he spotted me he looked around nervously then walked over to me. I held out my hand and said, "I'm Ricky."

"I know." he replied holding up my card as though to say that he had read it.

"And You are . . ." I asked.

He hesitated then replied, "I'm Andrew Collins."

Andrew," I repeated. Then it hit me like a bolt of lightning and I responded enthusiastically, "Andy! You're Andy." I was almost laughing from relief. "Boy am I glad to find you. Penny talks about you to my son, Jesse all the time. In fact when she isn't thinking she calls him Andy." Then I realized I was babbling. So I said, "I'm sorry. Please sit down. I have a million things to ask you."

Andy stayed standing as he replied, "No offense ma'am, but I have to be sure of who I'm talking to and I want to talk to Penny."

I was anxious to find out what he knew, but thought I understood his reluctance to talk to me too. I backed off a bit and said, "Okay, I know you must have your doubt. After everything that little girl has gone through you don't want to cause her anymore grief, am I right."

He replied with a stiff upper lip. "Something like that. Do I get to talk to her?"

"Yes," I answered, "If you don't mind coming up to my room where it's a little more private I'll place a call to her room right now."

Andy acted as though he was uncomfortable with the situation, but finally agreed. When we got to the room I dialed the phone immediately and waited. Room 345 please."

I waited again then I heard, "Hello."

"Jesse, its mom," I said excitedly, "is Penny awake?"

"He replied, "Yes, why?"

"You'll never guess who is sitting right here with me right now in my motel room," I said.

"Tell me something good mom. I could use some good news right now," Jesse answered.

"Oh this is good alright." I couldn't keep him in suspense any longer. "Jesse it's Andy."

"Oh Mom that's great! Just a minute I'll put Penny on the phone!" Jesse was excited as I heard him say to Penny. This call is for you Penny. My mom has a surprise for you."

Then I heard Penny's voice, "Hello."

"Hi Penny this is Ricky, Jesse's mom. Do you remember me," I asked.

"You're the lady who read to me," she replied.

"That's right Penny," I answered. "Now I have a surprise for you are you ready?"

"Yes ma'am," she replied.

"Okay, Here's the surprise." I said and I handed the phone to Andy.

Chapter Twenty-Three

Penny looked confused and Jesse was on pins and needles as he watched her face. Just then she heard a familiar voice, "Hey Penny Candy,"

Penny's face lit up brighter than Jesse had ever seen and he had to chuckle. As Penny burst out with, "Andy is that really you? Did you find my Daddy? Where are you?"

Andy replied, "Easy Penny I can only answer one question at a time. I'm in Beverly Hills with Ricky. Yes its really me and as for your father, I need to know if you want me to tell Ricky what I know. Is she okay?"

"She's Jesse's mom and she's trying to find Daddy for me. Jesse is my new friend. He's like you Andy."

Andy smiled, "That's good Penny candy. I'm glad you're safe. I'll help Ricky find your dad and we'll come and get you okay?"

"Okay, hurry Andy. I don't want grandpa to find me first." Penny got serious.

"We will Penny. Good-bye and I miss you."

"I miss you too. Good-bye."

Penny still held the receiver in her hand as she beamed at Jesse. "That was Andy."

Jesse chuckled, "Yes it was. Wasn't that a nice surprise?"

Penny shook her head yes, "You said your mother would find him and she did and now they're going to look for my daddy."

Jesse answered, "that's great Penny now let me talk to mom for a minute."

Penny handed Jesse the phone and Jesse said, "Mom are you still there?"

"Yes, Jesse. I'm still here," I replied.

"Penny says you and Andy are going to look for her father. Is that right," Jesse asked.

"I hope so. I'll let you know more later. Andy insisted on talking to Penny before he'd tell me anything, so I don't know yet."

"Okay mom, let us know as soon as you know anything okay?"

"I'll call Becky as soon as I can okay?"

"Okay, I'll talk to you soon I hope. Bye mom."

"Bye son and by the way thank you for taking such good care of Penny, but son be very careful okay."

"I will mom, Bye."

As I hung up the phone I sighed. "God I miss my kids," I said out loud without thinking.

Andy was more at ease now and asked, "How many kids do you have?"

I looked at him and smiled, "I have two wonderful young adults." Then I snapped back to reality. "So Now can I ask you some questions?"

Andy smiled and said, "Penny says you're okay so I'm ready to tell you what I know, but I must warn you that this could be dangerous."

I gave him a sarcastic look and said, "Do I look as though I have been on a cake walk. This case has already cracked three of my ribs and fractured my arm, say nothing about the bruises and cuts. I've been shot at and my cars been blown up. I've traveled half way across the country to find you. I'm not about to give up now. I promised that little girl I'd help her and I'm going to."

Andy shook his head in disbelief, "Well lady, far be it for me to stop you."

"Okay then sit down here and tell me what you know." I said. "I already know that Penny has been raped and molested by her grandfather, but I don't know who her grandfather is and I have no idea where to start looking for her father. By the way Penny said that you were an actor, so what where you doing mopping floors at the school today."

"Well it sounds as though you already know most of the story, but I'll tell you what I know," Andy began. First of all, I do work for an acting company, but it doesn't exactly pay the bills, so I take on other jobs to help supplement my income. I do pretty well. Anyway I met Penny at the school. She was always sitting by herself and I felt sorry for her so I started clowning around with her at lunchtime. Pretty soon we started hanging out together. She became like a little sister to me and her mom was always working so I kind of looked out for her what I could, when I was working in the area. She told me all of her darkest secrets and it broke my heart. I've been putting traces out for her dad ever since. Then one day Penny came to me and said that her grandfather was going to hurt me if I didn't stop looking for her dad and stay away from her. She was so scared that I backed off from the investigation, but I tried to see her in secret as much as possible."

I just shook my head as I listened to his story. "It's pretty much as I suspected," I remarked. "So do you know this grandfather?"

Andy shook his head and said, "All I know about him is that he is Blossom Johnson's stepfather that he kept them in that house to keep control over them and paid for Penny to go to that private school. Also that he is a U.S. Marshal or something."

I sat bolt upright in my chair at those words. "But you never heard his name?"

"No, never," Andy replied.

"Andy I have to make a phone call, for Penny's safety, can you hold on for just a minute?" I felt a sudden urge to warn Becky and my kids. Hicks was looking guiltier by the minute.

Andy nodded and I dialed the phone quickly. "Becky this is important. I'm sitting here with Andy," I said the second Becky answered the phone.

"You found him, that's great," she responded.

"Yes Becky, but listen. Andy says that Penny's grandfather is a U.S. Marshal." I stated.

"Oh my god," Becky replied. "Does that mean what I think it means."

"Its very possible Becky. You've got to get hold of Ned and get Penny and Jesse out of there right now. I want you and Annie out of there too. He could use you to get to them. Do you understand me." I was scared out of my wits for them.

"I understand Ricky. I'll get right on it. Ricky from now on call me on my cell phone okay?"

"I understand Becky, now get going. I'll call to check on you later."

"Okay, good-bye," she said and hung up quickly.

"Andy was tense when I got off the phone. "What was all of that about? Is Penny in danger?"

"I don't know, but I'm not taking any chances. There is a U.S. Marshal that arrived in town shortly after Penny's accident and kicked me off the case, but I'm stubborn. Anyway, He's got a colleague guarding Penny's room and I don't trust him."

Andy jumped to his feet. "He could be Penny's grandfather."

"I know," I replied, "but I have friends and family there and they're going to try to get Penny out of there and hide her until we can find out for sure and put a stop to him. Now I need you to tell me what you found out about Penny's father."

Just that his name is Peter Johnson and that he's a mechanic. I also found out that he moved to Redlands, when the grandfather drove him out. I don't know where in Redlands, but he shouldn't be too hard to find."

I placed my hand on Andy's shoulder, I'll find him."

Andy replied, "We'll find him. I promised Penny,"

"But what about your jobs," I asked.

"Penny's more important," he replied.

"Okay, Andy. Meet me here at seven o'clock tomorrow morning. We're going to Redlands."

Chapter Twenty-Four

After Becky got off from the phone with me she quickly dialed Kyle's number.

A sleepy Kyle answered the phone, "Hello"

"Kyle it's Becky. The hideout is a go. I've just heard from Ricky. Penny's grandfather is a U.S. Marshal."

Kyle jumped to his feet, "Meet me at the Hitching Post before opening in the morning."

"I'll be there. Meanwhile what do we do about Jesse and Penny?"

"I'll take care of that just meet me in the morning okay?"

"Okay, Bye."

"Good-bye."

Kyle threw on his clothes and called Ned to explain the situation. Ned replied, "You know what to do, Kyle. You know I can't move without Hicks knowing, so it's up to you. Meanwhile I'll distract Hicks when you're ready."

"Right Chief. I'm on it," Kyle replied and hung up."

"Next Kyle called Doctor Jenkins and informed him that he was taking a short fishing trip.

The doctor knew exactly what that meant. He called the hospital and ordered that Penny be taken down to the x-ray department at seven o'clock the next morning. Then he packed up some supplies and put them in his car and headed out of town.

Meanwhile Kyle called Annie and told her that her and her husband needed to take an emergency trip.

Annie knew exactly what to do. It meant that she and her husband would call work the next morning and say that I had a hunting accident and they had to leave town for a while. Then they would meet everyone at the cabin.

If all went well everybody would be safe by noon the next day."

The next morning Becky met Kyle before the Hitching Post opened and Kyle laid out the plan to her. Becky told him that she couldn't leave until Jake came in. She couldn't leave him without a waitress. Kyle informed her that she had no choice. He couldn't afford to leave anybody behind for Hicks to use to get to Penny.

Finally Becky agreed and went inside to call Jake.

Jake showed up a couple of minutes later. He agreed with Kyle that Becky needed to go right then and there and told her that he had called in a replacement and not to worry.

Then Kyle and Becky left in Kyle's van. Kyle pulled along beside the x-ray room with his bachelor's van as we all called it. It was perfect for transporting Penny because it had a bed in the back.

Doctor Jenkins showed up at the hospital just in time to set the plain in motion. He and a nurse and Becky all went to Penny's room. The Doctor told Jesse that Penny needed to go to x-ray, so he and Becky might as well go for a walk and stretch their legs.

Jesse looked confused by everyone's actions but agreed. He and Becky walked outside then Becky took him by the sleeve and said, "Don't ask any questions Jesse just go along with us and I'll explain on the way." They circled the hospital and hopped into Kyle's van. Just as they got in, the back door slid open and there was Doctor Jenkins with Penny in his arms. Jesse met him at the door and took Penny from him and laid her on the built in bed. Kyle started up the van and said, "See you there Doc."

The Doctor said, "I got everything set up out there lastnight. I'll be along soon."

The plan went like clockwork and they were off to the cabin without a hitch.

Annie called Becky on the cell phone and said that her husband had an out of town trip to go on anyway so he was just going to leave early, but that she was on her way to the cabin. They all met at the cabin and after they were all settled in Kyle left to return to town.

Penny was totally confused by all of the commotion, but Jesse told her that they were just moving her to someplace more comfortable to wait for her daddy.

"Your mom and Andy will bring him here," she asked.

"Yes Penny as soon as they find him," Jesse replied. "Now you rest while I talk to Annie for a minute okay?"

Penny shook her head. She seemed more at ease since they arrived at the cabin, which made Jesse more comfortable. Jesse walked out into the kitchen where Becky and Annie were standing and talking. He looked at them and said, "Does this mean that Hicks is Penny's grandfather?"

Becky replied, "It's very possible, Jesse." Then she explained my phone call to Jesse.

Jake was at the counter talking to Flo when Ned and Hicks walk into the Hitching Post, for their morning visit. Ned looked at Jake and said, "Good morning, Jake. Becky took the day off I see." He knew full well were Becky was, but he had to play the game and be convincing.

Jake knew also what Ned was up to so he replied, "You didn't hear Ned? Ricky has had a hunting accident and Becky and the kids have gone up there to be with her."

Becky went to the hospital to pick up Jesse this morning.

Just then Kyle walked in to the restaurant and sat next to Ned, as Hicks asked, "what kind of an accident?"

"We're not sure yet. Her Uncle just said that she had an accident and to hurry."

Hicks scratched his head and replied, "I wander what the girl is going to do without Jesse."

Just then Hicks' guard charge into the restaurant out of breath and in a panic. "She's gone! The girl is gone!"

Hicks jumped to his feet. Ned and Kyle did too and carried out their act. "What do you mean she's gone," Hicks demanded.

The guard explained that Penny was taken down to x-ray and that he waited outside the door for quite a while. Then after sometime he knocked on the door and nobody answered. When he stepped inside there was nobody there. The technician showed up right about then and said that he wasn't scheduled to do an x-ray for another half hour and that he didn't know anything about the girl."

Hicks turned to Ned. "Nothing had better have happened to that girl," he demanded.

Ned flared back, "She was your responsibility, remember. I was to mind my own business. Without Jesse with her someone probably figured it was time to make their move, whoever that somebody is. You know more about this than I do."

Hicks just shook his head angrily and ran out of the restaurant. Ned turned to Kyle and said, "we play this by the book just as though the kid is a missing person, okay"

Kyle nodded his head and headed back to the office, with Ned right behind him.

Chapter Twenty-Five

Andy and I left for Redlands in the morning hoping that all was well in Westfield. As we drove along we got to know each other better and I started to understand why Penny took to Jesse so quickly. He and Andy were quite a bit alike.

"Well Andy, this is quite a long drive to Redlands so we might as well get to know each other a little better. Tell me a little about yourself and your relationship with Penny," I said trying to break the silence as we got onto interstate ten heading east.

"There's not much to tell I'm afraid," He commented. "I'm twenty years old and a drama student. I never was very popular in school. Actually I was a bit of an outcast. I never was a jock or Mr. Popularity. I was the boy that got shoved around in the hallways. I guess that's why Penny caught my eye." Andy paused for a moment, then went on, "She didn't look as though she was comfortable around those Hollywood kids. She looked sad and so lonely sitting all by herself day after day. I just felt the need to put a smile on her face. Does that make sense to you?"

I smiled, "Yes it does."

"How did your son get through to her," he asked.

"Oh pretty much the same way," I replied. I explained the whole story to Andy how Penny wouldn't talk after the accident and how Jesse had stopped by to see me and started clowning around. Then I said, "I guess Jesse reminded Penny of you and she felt comfortable with that."

Andy smiled at that comment. "I can't wait to meet Jesse."

I said, "I know he can't wait to meet you either. He's really excited that I found you."

Andy nodded and said, "We'll find Penny's father too. I just know we will."

I replied, "I sure hope so. By the sounds, he's all she has to turn to now."

Andy stated, "No hoping about it. We're going to find him."

I chuckle and said, "Okay, we're going to find him." That sounded like something Jesse would have said and it tickled me to hear Andy say it.

Redlands was a good-sized town. I could tell that it was an upper classed town. Up in the foothills were several old but well cared for mansions mixed in with some newer but smaller homes. Down town was a quickly growing business district and we were sure that this was where we would find Penny's father. We stopped at a cute little restaurant

FEDERAL OFFENSE

to grab a bit to eat and I went to the local phone book to look up a Peter Johnson. At that point I was really wishing Johnson wasn't such a popular name. There were dozens of Johnson's. I decided I would call them all, which meant checking into a motel and settling down for hours with the phone stuck to my ear. This was the part of detective work that got on my nerves. It took time and patience, which were two things I had little of.

Meanwhile I had Andy in his room calling every garage in the yellow pages asking if they knew Peter Johnson.

Several hours later, as I was about to go completely out of my mind, Andy barged into the room. I've found him. He'll be getting off work in a little bit and we are to meet him at this address. He put a peace of paper down on the desk in front of me and stood there bouncing up and down.

He reminded me so much of Jesse at that moment that I had to laugh. "Okay," I said grabbing my jacket to cover my gun, "let's go."

As we pulled up in front of a quaint little corner lot surrounded by mansions on all sides I thought, what a peculiar place for a small home. Just then a truck pulled in behind us and a short, stocky, muscular man, with brown hair and grease covered clothes step out of it and walked up to my truck.

I stepped out and asked, "Are you Peter Johnson?"

"Who wants to know," he asked.

I showed him my card and my picture of Penny and said, "I'm working for the Westfield police department looking for the father of one Penny Johnson. She's in desperate need of her daddy."

Tears started to fill his eyes as he looked at Penny's picture. "My precious little girl," he said as he choked back the tears, "But where's Blossom? She should be with her mother."

I placed my hand on his shoulder and said, "Mr. Johnson is there someplace where we can sit down? We need to talk." I didn't know how much he knew about Penny's situation, but I had a feeling that what I had to tell him was going to put him in a tailspin and I wanted him seated.

He wiped his eyes and took a deep breath as he said, "Yes please come on in. This was my grandmother's place. She left it to me in her will. It's small but it's home. It use to be the servant's quarters for the mansion next door. My grand parents bought it several years ago. It was a house filled with love." He led Andy and I inside and we sat down. "Now what's going on here," he asked.

As carefully as possible I explained the situation to him. "Mr. Johnson, your wife was killed in a car accident, but Penny is safe with my children."

His shoulders sagged with grief as he heard the news. "What happened?"

"I believe she was running from her stepfather," I answered.

His body gave a jolt at the mention of the stepfather. "He runs her every thought. She wouldn't run from him. She's tied to him like a puppy on a leash."

"Mr. Johnson," I stated, "I need to ask you this and it's not going to be easy so brace yourself."

He gave me a curious look and asked, "What?"

I didn't want to ask what I had to ask next, but I took a deep breath and said, "Did you know that your wife and Penny were raped by the stepfather?"

He lunged to his feet in a fit of rage, "What are you saying? I'll kill him. My precious little Penny and . . . and Blossom raped."

Andy jumped to his feet and yelled, "Mr. Johnson, Penny needs you now. She's lost her mother and needs her father, not a raving lunatic."

Mr. Johnson stared at Andy for several moments then sunk back down into his chair. Then he looked at me with tear-filled eyes and said, "Take me to her."

"I will, but first I need to ask some questions," I stated.

"He nodded his head in understanding and said, "Go ahead."

I said, "Andy here says that your wife's stepfather is a U.S. Marshal, is that right?"

"Yes, that's right. He has a lot of power with the people around him. He can sweet talk his way into getting pretty much anything he wants and if that doesn't work he uses his power that comes with his badge."

I couldn't picture Hicks sweet-talking anybody, but pushing them around was certainly within his range of things. "Would his name happen to be Marshal Hicks?"

Johnson looked at me in disbelief and said, "No, Hicks is an idiot. He's with internal affairs. He's been trying to nail the old man for years, but has never managed to get so much as a dirt smudge on him. My father-in-law's name is Marshal Lee Grant."

Now I was in a tailspin. "Grant is Penny's grandfather." Then it hit me. I had shown Grant my license and gun permit. He knew where I was from and Penny was away from Hicks' protection. I jumped to my feet and said in a panic, "Where's your phone I have to make a call. Penny could be in real danger."

Johnson showed me to the phone and I quickly dialed Becky's cell phone. She was either in a dead spot or had the phone turned off either way I couldn't get through to her. I hung up the phone and dialed Ned's office. When Ned answered I didn't waste any time with explanations. I just said, "Ned tell Hicks that Grant knows where Penny is. Tell him to explain the whole thing to you. I'm on my way back with Penny's father right now. Then I hung up the phone.

Johnson and Andy both looked confused as Johnson asked, "How does he know where she is?"

"I'll explain while you pack," I said. We've got to get back there fast."

Just then the door barged open and Grant stood in the doorway with a gun in his hand, "Nobody's going anywhere," he stated, as he shut the door behind him.

Chapter Twenty-Six

As Ned hung up the phone he wondered how he was going to explain his, Kyle and Ricky's actions of late. Hicks had ordered Rick off the case the day he arrived. He, Kyle, Annie and Becky had lead Hicks to believe that Ricky was on a bear hunt with her Uncle Harry. Ned knew that Hicks was going to have his head for this. Ricky said that Grant was on his way to Westfield with such urgency in her voice. Grant was the U.S. Marshal that had come to Ricky's rescue twice that Ned knew of, so why was he coming to Westfield and what was so urgent about it? Ricky did say to have Hicks explain.

Ned took a deep breath and let it out slowly. Then he stepped out of his office and said what he had to say, before he had a chance to change his mind. "Marshal Hicks, I just got a strange but urgent call from Ricky."

Hicks looked up from his notes and said, "Oh? How is she doing after her accident?"

Ned replied to Hicks' question the only way he could, "Probably pretty sore right now, but I'll explain about that later. She has a message for you though."

Hicks gave Ned a curious look, as he asked, "What kind of message could Ricky possibly have for me?"

Ned braced himself for the storm that he knew was about to come and said, "I'm suppose to tell you that Marshal Grant knows where Penny is and you will explain to me what is meant by that."

Hicks' face turned red instantly and Ned could have counted every vessel and vein in his face. "I knew it," Hicks declared, "I just knew by the look on that woman's face that she wasn't about to drop Penny's case." Then he glared at Ned and continued, "and you, an officer of the law, blatantly disobeying my orders, is unforgivable."

Ned felt his own temper flaring as he retaliated. "Now look here," he stated, "Maybe we don't do thinks to your expectations in our little redneck town here, but we've managed to accomplish more than you have so far. Ricky has found Penny's friend, Andy and her father as well. She's on her way back here with them right now. What have you managed to do in the mean time, besides scare the hell out of that little girl and anger half of the town? Now what the hell is so urgent about Marshal Grant coming here?"

Hicks wasn't expecting Ned to stand up to him in that manner, which caused him to step back a little and stammer as he answered Ned's question. "Marshal Lee Grant is Penny's grandfather. You know the one that molested Penny and her mother."

Now Ned was caught off guard. He had firmly believed that Hicks was Penny's grandfather. Now he is told that the nice Marshal that had come to Ricky's rescue was actually the beast in question. Then he asked the burning question, "Then who are you and why are you even involved in this matter?"

Hicks wasn't use to having to explain himself, least of all to an overweight and definitely unprofessional, small town Police chief. This irritated him to no end, but he did answer Ned's question, "Lee Grant is a U.S. Marshal alright, but he believes that being a marshal make him above the law. I've been trying to get something on him for years, but he always manages to stay just one step ahead of me and comes out smelling like a rose."

Ned responded as though he had a bad taste in his mouth as he said, "So you're . . . Internal Affairs."

Hicks noticed Ned's obvious distaste, which really put him on the defensive, as he replied, "you act as though Internal Affairs is a bad thing, just like everyone else I meet up with, but with rogue cops like Grant out there setting his own agenda, what would you do?"

Ned thought about that for a moment and could think of no argument to that point. Finally he replied, "Well, now that we know where each other stands on the matter, do we work together to nail this creep or do we keep pulling against each other?"

"I don't know," Hicks replied, "It's rather pointless right now, with the girl missing."

"Well . . ." Ned said in an apprehensive manner. "Not exactly missing."

Hicks glared at Ned. "What do you mean by 'not exactly'. She's either missing or she's not missing and she's not in her hospital room . . ." Then he studied Ned a moment then said, "Don't tell me . . . another one of your hair brained schemes."

Ned nodded his head nervously, "I moved her to a safe place when we found out that Penny's grandfather was a U.S. Marshal and with you not being open with us about your intentions, I got worried for the child's safety. The Doctor, Becky, Jesse and Annie are with her."

"Where," Hicks demanded.

Ned was uneasy about telling Hicks very much, but at this point he didn't know whom to trust. He figured seeing I had told him to tell Hicks about Grant, that he might as well tell Hicks everything he knew. I have then hidden in my uncle's cabin out in Green Oaks, that's a pretty isolated spot north of town. Not many people know about it."

Hicks thought for a moment. He was at a loss as to how to make Penny any safer. "Okay," he said finally, "Who knows that they are out there?"

Ned ran the question over in his mind. "Well there's Jake, the owner of the Hitching Post. Then there's Annie's husband, but he's out of town on business." He searched his mind a while longer then finished his list, "Kyle and Ricky of course."

FEDERAL OFFENSE

Hicks pondered the situation a while longer then said, "Well, let's just keep things the way they are for now." He shook his head in disbelief at the situation that he had found himself in. Then he said, "Well obviously Ricky isn't on a bear hunt with her Uncle Harry, so you'd better tell me everything she has done since she left here. I need to know every detail." He looked at Ned with a look that meant, don't leave anything out.

Ned shook his head and took a deep breath. "This could take a while," he said, "so you might as well have a seat. She's been a busy girl."

At the cabin Jesse had built a fire in the fireplace and helped Penny walk out to the couch. It was a slow process, but soon Penny was curled up on the couch next to Jesse and had her head resting on his lap. Penny looked so contented lying there, that Jesse had to smile as he gentle stroked her soft blonde hair.

Annie and Becky were sitting across the room in the two stuffed recliners. As they sat there relaxing they watched Penny and Jesse with big grins on their faces.

Doctor Jenkins was sitting on the polished brick landing in front of the fireplace, poking at the fire with a stick. He turned a bit, looked over at Jesse and Penny and smiled. "Well Jesse," he said. "It looks to me as though you have someone there who will admirer you for life."

Jesse got a loving grin on his face and replied, "believe me Doc, I've done a whole lot worse in the past."

Annie chuckled and said, "Yah, I can remember vividly some of those losers you brought home and mom biting her tongue raw trying not to say anything until you saw for yourself what they were really like."

Jesse looked up at his sister with a playful grin on his face, as he said, "now easy Sis. I can remember a couple of winners that you dated in high school and mom doing a little tongue biting over them too."

Becky had to laugh at the two of them. She had only raised one child, so she had never witnessed sibling teasing. She was amused as she said, "Now children, I have no experience at refereeing these things and your mother isn't here to show me how it's done, so let's not have any bloodshed. Okay?"

Jesse stuck out his lower lip as though he was pouting. Then he said, "Okay Becky. I'll behave myself."

Penny rolled over a bit so that she could look up at Jesse. She had an amused look on her face as she said, "Jesse you're so silly sometimes."

Jesse looked down at her as he pretended to be totally shocked at her comment and he replied, "who me? Silly? Not me. I'm as serious as a heart attack."

Penny readjusted her position and snuggled up even closer to Jesse as she said in a contented voice, "I wish we could stay here like this forever."

Jesse continued stroking Penny's hair as he replied, "I wish we could too Penny. It's nice and cozy here, with the fireplace burning and being surrounded by nothing but love."

Annie commented, "That's the way life should always be, no pain, no hatred, just love."

Becky and Doctor Jenkins both nodded their agreement to Annie's comment.

Just then there was a knock at the cabin door and everybody sat up straight as though they were ready to scatter and hide. They all looked at each other with panicked looks on their faces. The serenity they had all felt just seconds earlier was replaced with horror as they imagined the worst.

Then they heard Kyle's voice call out to them. "It's only me."

Everyone settled back and let out a sigh of relief. Becky got up and unlocked the door to let Kyle in. He had a look of deep worry on his face as he stepped in the door. He looked toward Annie, Becky and the doctor and said, "Let's step out into the kitchen for a moment. We need to talk." Then he looked toward Jesse with a look that told him to keep Penny occupied.

Everybody knew by the look on Kyle's face that whatever he had to tell them wasn't good. They all got up and followed Kyle to the kitchen, leaving Jesse to sit with Penny by the fire.

Annie was worried. After all that had happened lately her first thought was that I might have gotten into another scrape. When the door closed behind them Annie looked at Kyle and asked, "is it mom? Is she alright?"

Kyle placed his hand on Annie's shoulder reassuringly and replied, "the last I heard from her she was fine, Annie. She and Andy have found Penny's father and are headed here to reunite them."

"Well that's good," Annie said, but Kyle's face was still tense, so she asked, "isn't it?"

"There's something else," Kyle added, "This is the part that bothers me."

Becky's curiosity was getting to her as she said, "So what is it Kyle? Stop the suspense and come out with it."

Kyle replied, "I'm trying to." Then he took a deep breath and said, "Penny's grandfather is not Marshal Hicks, it's Marshal Grant. You know the one that so conveniently shows up *just* in time to come to Ricky's rescue, every time that she's in trouble? Anyway, Ricky seems to think that he may be on his way here to get Penny."

Annie stiffened up as she thought out loud, "If Grant is Penny's grandfather then who is Hicks and what is his roll in all of this?"

Kyle got a sour look on his face as he answered, "He's Internal Affairs."

Becky responded with, "Then Hicks is here to get Grant and to protect Penny. I could have sworn that he was our monster.

Kyle nodded. "Me too. Now Ricky has practically handed Grant to Hicks on a silver platter. If he plays his cards right he'll have him. He should be grateful to Ricky for all of her help."

Annie was puzzled, "Well isn't he grateful?"

Kyle shrugged his shoulders and replied, "I don't think so. I think he's still irritated with her for not dropping the case when he ordered her to. I know that he's angry with Ned and I for our involvement."

Doctor Jenkins listened to the whole conversation with great interest as he shook his head in disbelief. "Some people refuse to admit when they're wrong. They would rather get angry and blame somebody else for their shortcomings."

Just then Jesse slipped quietly into the kitchen.

Annie turned to her brother with a concerned look on her face and asked, "Where's Penny?"

Jesse replied, "Don't worry. She's sound asleep on the couch with a contented smile on her face." As he walked over to the huddle he asked, "So what's going on out here?"

Annie quickly updated her brother and he replied, "Grant doesn't know anything about this cabin does he?"

Kyle shook his head. "No Jesse, how could he?"

"Good," Jesse replied, "Then we're better off here anyway. The hospital would be the obvious place to look."

"That's true," Kyle said thoughtfully.

"Yes Becky added, "But Grant always seems to show up wherever Ricky is, that's what's freaky." Then a look of horror slowly crept across Becky's face and she let out a gasp.

Annie looked curiously at Becky and asked, "What is it Becky? You look like you've seen a ghost."

Becky grabbed Kyle by the sleeve and stated in an urgent tone, "He's not coming here, at least not just yet. He's going after Ricky first. If he knows every move that Ricky makes, then he knows that she's found Penny's father. He has no choice. He has to find a way to silence them first."

Chapter Twenty-Seven

Staring down the barrel of a loaded gun had never been one of my favorite positions to be in, so a cold chill ran down my spine as I stared down the barrel of this one. Especially because it was being wielded by a half crazed U.S. Marshal. I had finally put it all together. Grant was crazy, but he worked in a cool and calculating manner. This made him more dangerous than most. My mind was working overtime trying to figure a way out of the mess we were in. I had to think of Andy and Johnson's safety. Penny needed them both in order to have a chance of healing some of the emotional scars.

Just then I noticed somebody slip in the door behind Grant and close it quietly behind Grant. My senses heightened even more as I recognized Angel standing there like a second shadow behind Grant. He was also holding a gun. This made the situation even more complicated. I could feel my own gun snug in its holster, but this was not the time or place for a shootout, so I didn't go for it. Knowing it was there was enough for the time being. I couldn't figure out the relationship between Angel and Grant. Obviously Angel and Lou were Grants Henchmen, but if they were loving brothers, why would Angel be tied to Grant's shirttail now? Grant was the one that killed Lou. Finally I decided Grant made up that story for my benefit, to see if I would equate it to Penny and tell him all about her. I was glad that I hadn't completely fallen for his act. I could have handed Penny right over to him, without even knowing it. Whatever the reason Angel was with Grant and we were in deep trouble. That much I knew for sure. Although, thinking back on my experience with Angel and Lou, Angel seemed to be the unwilling follower.

Grant stepped forward and demanded, "Everybody sit down. We're going to have a little chat about my granddaughter." Then he glanced at Angel and chuckled, "Isn't this a cozy little situation we've got here. There's the loving Daddy, the nosy friend and the private eye, all in one place, ready to go riding in to rescue poor little Penny."

Angel seemed to fidget a bit as he smiled and said, "Yes sir, cozy in deed, a regular family affair." I began to realize that Angel wasn't a big threat. If I could find a way to disarm Grant, I believed Angel would fold.

Suddenly Grant's mood shifted and he got a serious look on his face. He bent down and stared straight at me. "Now you're going to tell me exactly where you have hidden my granddaughter or I'm going to have to make you talk." He squinted his eyes and continued. "Believe me, Lou has nothing on me when it comes to making people talk, especially women. I have much more fun forcing women to talk." Then he got an evil grin on his face as he rubbed my cheek with the back of his hand.

I glared at him and turned my head enough to make him move his hand. Then I said in a defiant manner, "Is that suppose to scare me?" It did scare the hell out of me, because I knew what he had in mind and it made me sick to think of it. If I let it show how scared I was, Grant would know that he had the upper hand and I couldn't let that happen, so I turned to Johnson and winked at him and said, with a sarcastic grin on my face, "Gee he thinks he's a big man now."

Grant's face turned instantly red and the blood vessels in his temples looked as though they were ready to explode. All of a sudden he gripped my arm so tight that I thought it would break and yanked me out of the chair so hard that it took a second or two for my feet to find the ground. He pulled me in closer to him and said, "Let me show you just how big of a man I am and how insignificant you are." He slammed me up against the bedroom door like a rag doll and held me there while he turned the handle. Then after opening the door he literally lifted me off from my feet and threw me through the air. I landed with a hard jolt onto the hardwood floor. Grant slammed the door behind him as I tried to scramble to me feet. Then he grabbed me again as he picked me up off from the floor and slammed me down onto the bed pinning my arms with his powerful grip. Then he looked deep into my eyes. I was sure that he was looking for the fear he needed me to show, so I glared at him, still trying to show defiance, on my part.

He gripped my wrists even tighter as he declared, "We can do this the hard way or we can do this the easy way. It's all up to you. Personally I hope you chose the hard way. I'd enjoy making you talk." Once again he got that evil grin on his face.

A very real flash of fear ran through me, which I hoped Grant couldn't detect. I knew that he was a very muscular man. There was no possibly way I could fight him off if he did what it looked like he was about to do. Instinctively I brought my leg up with as much force as I possible could for the position I was in. I knew I couldn't have connected too hard, but it most have been enough to get his attention, because he backed off quickly and stared at me for a moment. Then he moved more cautiously as he pulled out his handcuffs and hand cuffed me to the bed as he announced, "Don't worry honey. I'll get back to you later." Then he winked at me as he said in a cocky manner, "I always save the best for last. Right now I need to settle up with the two losers in the livingroom as he opened the door and left it open, while he entered the livingroom. I figured that he wanted me to be able to witness whatever he was about to do.

"Now," Grant said in an almost lecturing voice. "As for you two I thought that I made it *extremely* clear to the both of you that my girls were off limits.

Johnson's rage could be heard clearly in his voice as he said, "Blossom was my wife and Penny is my daughter. I left because I felt unwanted, that's all. I've never been afraid of you."

"Is that right, Mr. Grease monkey," Grant said in a sarcastic voice. Then his voice changed to anger as he said, "then try this on for size." Then I heard a gunshot and Johnson yelling out in excruciating pain. My heart went up in my throat and I started yanking at the cuffs that held me to the bed. I yelled out to Grant, "It's me you want, you son of a bitch, not them. They don't know where Penny is, but I do."

Johnson yelled out from the livingroom. "Don't tell him anything, Ricky. I'd rather die than to let this creep hurt my baby again."

Grant laughed as though what Johnson said amused him, then he said, "well, isn't that touching. Well guess what, I'm not going to kill you, because you're going to jail for kidnapping and child rape." Then he stepped back so I could see him and motioned toward both Andy and me, as he continued, "and you two are accessories after the fact."

Johnson was both angry and disgusted as he yelled, "how can I go to jail for kidnapping my own daughter. Her mother is dead."

The news of Blossom's death didn't even seem to phase Grant as he continued, "Oh that's easy to explain," Grant replied with great satisfaction in his voice. "I convinced the courts six months ago that Blossom wasn't mentally stable enough to have custody of Penny. It wasn't hard, because she's always been weak and of course poor Penny's father wasn't in the picture. The natural thing to do was to give custody to Penny's loving grandfather. Of course I volunteered to look after Blossom too. It was the only responsible thing to do." Grant shook his head and continued. "Who would have ever guessed that Blossom would have gotten the gumption to defy me the way she did and run off with Penny." Then he glared at Johnson, "So you see, I have all the right in the world to arrest you."

At this point, Andy spoke up. "When the world hears that it was you and not Mr. Johnson that did all of those terrible things to Blossom and Penny, we'll be exonerated anyway."

I cringed as I thought, "Oh Andy please don't say anything. You'll direct his anger toward you."

Just then I noticed Grant raising his gun up into position, so I tried to distract him by shouting, "That's right too many people already know the truth." I had to direct Grant's attention away from Andy, so I continued, "How do you plan to silence everybody?"

Grant glanced back into the bedroom at me and grinned a satisfied grin. "I don't have to silence anybody. My granddaughter will say whatever I want her to say when I'm done with her. You know, she really loves her grandpa and her daddy does bad things to her, so grandpa takes care of her."

I wanted to say something to shut him up for good, but I also knew that I couldn't say anything to reveal where Penny was hidden or let on to the trap that I hoped was waiting for him at the other end. I decided to say nothing and let him think he'd won.

That was the first time I had really notices the hand gun Grant was wielding. It was a gold colored semi-automatic fifty caliber, with a six inch barrel. Just the right gun for an egotistical man like Grant. A gun like that could have done some major damage to Johnson's leg.

Grant was tired of torturing Johnson and said, "You're no challenge at all. You never have been." Then he turned to Angel and gave him his orders, "Keep these boys out of trouble for me. I've got unfinished business in the other room." He stepped back into the bedroom and focused his attention on me. "I'd rather deal with a feisty woman, any day, than two weak men." Then he closed the bedroom door. "Now little lady, it's time for you and me to have a little fun." He reached for his keys and undid the cuffs. While doing so he pulled my gun from the holster and through it onto the floor.

As soon as my hands were free I began swinging. Grant quickly slammed his fist up under my chin, with a powerful blow, which rattled my brain. As I lay there trying to recover he grabbed up both of my wrists and pinned them over my head with his left hand, as he smiled and said, "Yes ma'am, this is going to be more fun than I thought." Then he started undoing my belt as he continued, "I've wondered ever since the day I met you, what it would be like with a scrapper. Now I know that I'm going to enjoy this."

Chapter Twenty-Eight

Marshal Hicks found himself in a position that he had always sworn he wouldn't be in. He had to rely on others to succeed in catching Grant. For years now he had worked alone. This small town police chief was right about one thing. He hadn't gotten anywhere on his own and a barely qualified private detective had managed to blow the case wide open. It infuriated Hicks to come to this realization, as he thought to himself, *a middle-aged housewife playing detective stumbles onto the answers in no time and I've done everything by the book for years using all of the proper steps and got zilch.* He slammed his note pad down unto the desk.

Ned was standing at the coffeepot and when Hicks connected with the desk, Ned spun around with his hand gripping the butt of his revolver. "Damn Hicks, the tension is too thick around here already! Don't do that! I could have shot you."

Hicks just snickered, "You'd have never cleared leather."

Ned had just about had it with Hicks' superior attitude. "Why don't you go to hell?"

I'm already there," Hicks snarled as he stood up and stepped outside for some fresh air.

Ned shook his head as he watched Hicks pacing on the front step of the police station and mumbled mostly to himself; "No you just bring it with you wherever you go."

A young officer that was standing nearby during the whole scene almost choked on his coffee as he heard Ned's words.

Ned looked at the young man and said, "That's what pride does to you boy. If you don't want to end up like him you'll swallow your pride to get the job done."

The young officer nodded his head and said, "Yes Chief, I'll remember that." Then he went back to his desk.

Just then Kyle started to walk by Ned when Ned said, "Kyle do you know why I picked Ricky for this case?" He felt the need to explain his actions and Hicks wasn't about to listen.

Kyle looked puzzled, as he replied, "No chief. I sure was curious when you did that, but she did turn out to be the best person for the job."

"Well Ricky told me one time about her childhood, Ned stated. "I guess you didn't know that she was abused as a child."

Kyle replied, "No I didn't."

FEDERAL OFFENSE

"Well it seems that Ricky was taken away from her father after her mother died and was put into a foster home," Ned explained. "These people were real good at making people believe that they were loving foster parents. Even Ricky's own family thought they did wonders with Ricky. Little did anybody no that she was beaten often for ridiculous reasons, like breaking a dish or smiling at a boy. When she did get up enough courage to tell people, they said that she was lying and a troublemaker. Her own aunts and uncles wouldn't even believe her. The foster parents called her a slut half of the time and always told her she was stupid. Haven't you ever wondered why Ricky insisted that her children knew that she was proud of them and that they can do anything they set their minds to?"

Kyle answered, "Yes Annie and I were talking about that just a while ago."

Because she never wanted them to feel like she did growing up and that's why I knew that she'd fight for Penny as well," Ned continued. "After I found out that Penny had been molested, I knew that the child probably went through years of torture and was convinced that nobody would believe her if she told, much less fight for her. Ricky was to only answer."

As Ned and Kyle talked, Hicks continued pacing the step for quite some time then took his radio off from his belt and spoke into it. Wilder how's it looking out there?"

"Peaceful so far sir," came a voice from the radio.

"No sign of Grant," Hicks asked.

"No sir," returned the voice.

"Damn," Hicks replied, "Stay on your toes. I'll be out to relieve you soon."

"Yes sir," the voice answered.

Hicks walked back into the station, where Ned was carrying a serious conversation with Kyle. When Kyle spotted Hicks he turned to Ned and said, "I think I understand a lot more now Chief. Thanks for telling me." Then he turned and walked away quickly.

Hicks walked up to Ned and said in an irritated tone, "are you sure that Ricky has any idea what she's doing? There's no sign of Grant yet."

Ned tried to hold his feeling back as he said, "All I know is what she told me on the phone and she was there in the thick of things, so she ought to have a pretty good idea what's going on." Then he said, "Of course Kyle seems to think . . ."

Hicks interrupted, "That's the trouble with you Chief, you listen to everybody's hair brained ideas and you have everybody out there doing their own thing and us in here chasing our tails. This is exactly why I didn't want any of you involved. Now I have a bunch of half baked idiots running the show and I'm standing here waiting to pick up the pieces."

Ned just shook his head and walked to his office mumbling to himself, "More like waiting to take the credit."

"What's that," Hicks asked in a sharp tone.

Ned sneered at Hicks and said, "I said, 'that must be it'." Then he stepped into his office and slammed the door behind him.

Hicks mumbled to himself as he walked out of the station house and got into his car. "Small town mentality, I just love it."

All of the way out to the lookout he had established, he reassured himself that he knew what he was doing and that everyone else was small minded and ignorant. By the time that he reached Wilder he was back to his over confident self. "Well how's the nature watch going Wilder," he asked as he strutted up to one of the young Marshals that had been guarding Penny in the hospital.

"No change sir," the young man replied.

"I didn't think so," Hicks replied. "We're out here playing game warden, because some frustrated woman that's going through a mid-life crisis thinks she's a detective."

The young officer didn't react to the statement. He just said, "Yes sir."

Hicks, feeling rather pleased with himself said, "You can go now Wilder."

"Yes sir," the young man replied and left Hicks to bask in his own self-confidence.

Chapter Twenty-Nine

As Grant was trying to undo my belt, I was fighting him for all that I was worth. He might get his way with me but not without paying a high price.

All the time this was going on I was flashing back to a time in my life when I was about fifteen and a boy I worked with that thought that I was playing with his affections. I use to sit and talk to him on breaks about my boyfriend, which was another guy we use to work with, before he went in the army. I thought we were friends, but he thought I was teasing him. He and two of his friends caught me walking home from work late one night and took turns with me. The worst part was that I knew I couldn't talk about it to anybody, because my foster parents believed that I was a slut anyway. I knew they would say that I asked for it. I had to just keep it bottled up inside and not say a word. It made me angry and bitter and I always swore that no man would even violate me again like that, now here I was fighting someone off again and knowing that I was going to lose. I thought about Penny and if I felt this helpless, then how must she have felt? She was so tiny and her grandfather was such a big man muscular man.

Just then we heard diesel engines and air horns. Grant jumped to his feet and ran to the front room to look outside. He stepped back into the doorway, looked at me and said, "That's all right, I hear there's a younger version of you in Westfield. It will be a real pleasure to have that." He spun around and yelled to Angel, then they ran out the back door.

I jumped to my feet snatched up my gun and ran after them. I got a shot off and I saw his shoulder flinch as they ran down the alley.

I turned and ran back into the house just as Dave charged through the front door.

I looked at him and said, "I've never been so glad so see anybody in my whole life as I am to see you right now."

Then I turned my attention to Johnson and Andy. Grant's shot had hit Johnson in the leg and Andy was applying pressure to it. "How bad is it," I asked.

"It just grazed me. I don't think it's too bad. I'll live," Johnson replied. "We've got to get to my little girl before he does."

"Penny is well hidden for now, I said. "We'll take the next flight out after you're taken care of."

Then I turned back to Dave; "You'll never know how grateful I am that you showed up when you did." I was trembling by now and my legs were a little week. How did you know where to find me?"

Kyle got through to Janice and told her that Becky believed that Grant was coming after you first. Janice called her sister in Los Angeles and she radioed me. I called in a few friends along the way, which reminds me we'd better get our rigs out of here. He put his hand on my shoulder and asked, "Are you going to be alright?"

"Yes," I replied, "but before you go could you help me load Johnson here into my truck?"

"Sure," he replied and he and Andy helped Johnson to the truck.

Once we got Johnson comfortable I thanked all of the guys and told them they were welcome at my place any time. Then I gave Dave a hug and said, "Thank Janice for me please. You two have turned out to be my guardian angels and I'll never forget what you've done."

Johnson had come out of it very lucky. The bullet had just taken a bit of meat out of the side of his leg, so after being treated and answering a few questions to the local authorities, Johnson was fitted with crutches and we were on our way. Once we were on the plane I didn't know who was more anxious to get to Westfield, Johnson or me. We both wanted to stop Grant before he got to Penny, but I had another worry as well. My kids were there and in danger, especially Annie.

Johnson looked at me. "What did he mean by that last comment?"

"My kids are with Penny, I replied. "He meant that seeing that he didn't get his way with me, he'd get my daughter, Annie." Then I stated as I shook with rage, "I'll kill him, I swear I will."

Andy commented, "Careful Ricky your anger can get you killed."

"Not before I blow his head off," I answered.

Chapter Thirty

As Grant and Angel fled the house in Redlands, Angel noticed Grant stagger a bit from my shot. Grant picked up speed and passed up Angel. Angel saw his chance to escape and turned off from the alley and hid behind a dumpster. He waited to see if Grant would return. After several minutes he started to breathe easier. Maybe Grant had stepped into it too deep this time and he would finally be free of him.

He thought back on the day Grant caught him standing on the street corner buying a stolen watch from Lou and arrested him for being a fence and Lou for being a jewel thief. He didn't know Lou at the time and had no idea the watch was stolen or even if it was, but Grant had him scared. After that every time Grant had a dirty job to do he forced him and Lou into doing it for him or he's put them away. Later he learned that Lou had murder charges on him and this scared Angel. He had seen Lou do some pretty horrible things, but shooting that trucker was totally uncalled for and made Angels stomach turn. The man didn't even put up a fight. Granted he didn't answer any of Lou's questions, but murder was not within Angel's range of capabilities. Lou had a temper that was almost always out of control. This made him very useful to Grant. Angel had always been sent along with Lou, he guessed to be the cool headed one. He hated the whole thing but Grant had enough on him by now that there was no turning back. Before long the charges were out of this world.

When Grant killed Lou, Angel realized how dispensable he was too. There was no love lost between him and Lou, but Lou's death was enough to scare Angel. He knew that as soon as it was convenient to Grant he'd be dead as well, but where do you hide from a U.S. Marshal. Angel didn't know, but he was sure going to try. He took off running. He was going to get as far away from Redlands as possible, before Grant realized he was missing. He also knew that Grant was headed for Westfield next so he figured to go toward Los Angeles. Maybe he could hide out in the back alleys. If he stayed to himself and kept his mouth shut he might just be able to hide out long enough for Grant to forget about him or mess up enough to get caught or killed.

He knew that even if Grant was caught or killed the charges against him would still be pending and he'd never totally be free, but not having to deal with Grant again would be enough for him for now.

After Grant fled from the house in Redlands and did his best to plug the whole in his shoulder he got on the radio and called for a jet to meet him at the old Norton Airbase outside of San Bernardino. Angel had gotten separated from him during their escape, but Grant wasn't worried. Angel knew that Grant would track him down sooner or later and if he wanted to stay out of jail, he'd do as he was told.

Grant met the plane and was off within hours. While on the plane he changed into a flannel shirt and jeans. He needed to blend in as much as possible. The plane landed at another old airstrip on the edge of town. Working his way through the shadows he finally found the Police Station.

By now he had figured out that Hicks was in Westfield and knew that if he was patient Hicks would lead him straight to Penny. He figured that Hicks was so arrogant that he didn't believe that he could slip up. Grant had used Hicks' arrogance against him many times in the past. Grant smiled as he thought of making a fool out of Hicks again, but he was growing tired of Hicks nipping at his heel all of the time to. Maybe this time he'd just eliminate him all together.

The hours passed and Grant waited. He believed that he had plenty of time, because Johnson's wound would slow us down considerably, besides he would have us arrested the minute we showed up. He had already called into headquarters and reported that I had kidnapped Penny and was after him. Of course he didn't tell why I was after him.

After several hours Grant saw his opportunity. Wilder, Hicks' assistant, left the police station and headed north out of town. Grant flagged down a cab and said, "Head north. I'll tell you when to stop."

Old Ralph the cab driver didn't recognize the man in his cab, so he said, "From out of town, ah? Visiting friends?"

"Something like that," Grant replied.

"Not many people use these cabins out here this time of year, except the chief of police." Ralph continued. "He hides out in his uncle's cabin once in a while and leaves Kyle to hold down the fort. He doesn't think anybody knows about this place, but not much gets by old Ralph here."

Just then Grant noticed that Wilder had pulled off from the road and started climbing up a hillside. "This will be fine right here," Grant said and Ralph pulled over.

"That's strange the chiefs not using the cabin this week and there's smoke coming from the chimney."

Grant looked around and spotted the cabin with the smoke coming out. He grinned and then said, "what do I owe you?"

Ralph replied, "Two dollars," then he asked, "Friend of the Chief's?"

Grant smiled, "Friend of a friend, you might say." He paid Ralph and waited for him to drive out of sight. Then he walked back to where he had seen Wilder start up the hillside.

Slowly he worked his way up in the same direction and before long he heard Hicks' voice. "You know Wilder I don't think Grant is going to show. I think once again that slimy snake has slipped through the cracks. I knew Ricky was leading us on a wild goose chase."

Grant chuckled to himself then slipped away toward the car Wilder had arrived in and waited in the shadows for Hicks to come down the hill. He didn't have to wait for long for Hick to saunter down the hill mumbling to himself.

Grant stepped out from behind Hicks as he drew out a knife. "Slimy snake hah?"

Hicks spun around and reached for his gun as Grant thrust the knife deep into his chest. "You lose again," He said as Hicks' gun fired as he sunk to the ground and curled up in a ball from the pain. He mumbled, "Grant, it can't be." Then he quit breathing and went limp.

Grant kicked Hicks' dead body and chuckled, "Loser." Then he got a look of delight on his face as he said aloud to himself, "Now Penny, my little precious it's time to come home with Grandpa, but first I'll show you how it's done with an older girl. Maybe you'll learn something." The thought of it got his heart pumping rapidly as he headed toward the cabin that held the children.

Jesse and Penny lazed on the couch watching the fire while Becky and Annie nodded off in their chairs. Doctor Jenkins had gone home for the night and everyone was exhausted from a day of worry.

Just then the cabin door flew open as the door jam splintered from the force and Grant stepped inside, "Surprise, it's grandpa." He was wielding a gun and counting heads. "You're all under arrest for kidnapping."

Penny flew into Jesse's arms, while Annie and Becky shot to their feet. Grant looked at Annie and said with an evil grin on his face, "You and I have a little business to attend to, but first . . . You . . ." He looked at Becky and through her two sets of cuffs. One for you and one for our night in shining armor here. Then the both of you sit over in these chairs and behave yourselves."

He watched as Becky obeyed. All of the time that Becky was following Grant's instructions she kept wondering where Hicks was. When was he going to charge in there in save them? This was his big moment of glory so what was he waiting for?

Chapter Thirty-One

When we got to the airport I hurried to the front door and spotted Ralph the cab driver, just pulling in. I flagged him down franticly as Johnson and Andy caught up with me. I said, "Boy am I glad to see you Ralph. We need a ride to Ned's cabin."

Ralph nodded his head as we climbed into the cab. Then he said, as he looked at me in the rearview mirror, "Damn Ricky, did you get the bear or did the bear get you?"

"So far it's a draw," I replied. Then I said, "Hurry Ralph it's important. I promise nobodies going to give you a ticket tonight."

Ralph sped up a little then commented, "That's an awful busy place tonight. What are you folks doing out there?"

I tensed up at Ralph's words, "What to you mean, that it's a busy place out there tonight?"

"Well I just got back from taking a man out there," Ralph replied. "He was an odd sort but he said that he was a friend of a friend."

I glanced at Johnson and Andy. They both sat forward at these words. "Ralph," I said, "That was no man that was a monster. Give this old bucket of bolts everything you've got. My kids are out there and that monster wants to have his way with Annie and this man's little girl."

Ralph floored the accelerator, as he said, "Not Annie! Why didn't you say so? Hold on folks, we're going to fly."

Ralph was an old stock car driver from way back and this night he showed us that it was still in his blood, as we slid around corners and whipped around straight again. As we neared Ned's hideaway, I spotted Hicks' car and a young Deputy Marshal, on the side of the road using the radio. I grabbed Ralph's shoulder, "Stop here." I threw a five at him and said, "go tell Ned and Kyle what's happening.

Then the young Marshal said and tell them Hicks is dead."

Ralph nodded and sped away and I ran up to the Marshal that seemed completely out of it. I grabbed him by the front of the shirt and shook him hard. "Where is Grant," I demanded.

The young officer just mumbled, "I don't know."

FEDERAL OFFENSE

I shoved away from him and started running frantically toward Ned's cabin, as I shouted back to Johnson and Andy, "you two stay here." I pulled my gun from my holster and prayed that I wasn't to late.

It seemed as though my legs were moving in slow motion. I feel my heart beating so hard could feel it in every part of my body. I stumbled and fell, skidding across the ground as the gun flew from my hand. Fanatically I felt around in a panic. After what seemed like eternity I found it and got back to my feet, taking of running again. All the way I prayed that I wasn't too late.

Once Becky and Jesse were seated in the chairs, Grant turned his attention to Annie and Penny. "Penny, Come to grandpa," he demanded. "You've been a bad little girl."

Penny stood up stiffly, but froze where she stood.

Grant grabbed Penny and stood her at the end of the couch as he kept the gun pointed at Annie. "If anybody objects, the school teacher gets it."

Jesse's muscles tightened with rage, but he feared for his sister's life, so he could do nothing.

Grant proceeded to remove Penny's clothing and said, "Now Penny, you've never managed to get it right, so I'm going to show you how a real woman takes it."

Penny stood at the end of the couch trembling all over, but never shed a tear, as she nodded that she understood.

Then Grant turned to Annie. "Your mom and I had quite an interesting moment earlier. She was quite a scrapper how about you." He grabbed Annie and through her down onto the couch.

Annie was no easy mark. My girl had always seemed mellow, but deep down inside there was a tiger in her, when threatened and Grant got a taste of that tiger in short order as Annie clawed his face with her razor sharp nails.

Jesse also sprung into action. He may have had his hands cuffed behind his back but his feet were free and as Grant turned his head from Annie's clawing, Jesse nailed him in the face with his size thirteen's. With both Annie clawing and punching him and Jesse kicking him Grant most have thought that he disturbed a hornet's nest. Finally he staggered backward and got off a shot, which crazed Jesse's cheek. Jesse stumbled backward and Annie froze as Grant said, "I've about had it with you," and he leveled the gun preparing to finish Jesse off.

Just then several shots came from the opened doorway, blowing out the side of Grant's head, as I stepped inside and said, "burn in hell sucker." I had emptied my gun on him in seconds.

Just then Ned, Kyle, Wilder, Johnson and Andy all arrived on the scene. Johnson paused at Grant's body for a second then grabbed his shivering naked daughter up into his arms, while letting his crutches drop to the floor. He grabbed the blanket off from the couch and wrapped it around her. "Daddy's here now honey. You're safe."

Annie through her arms around me while Kyle removed Jesse and Becky's cuffs and we all hugged.

"Thank god you got here when you did, mom," Annie cried.

I smiled in a sad manner and said, "Mess with my kids and die." Then I hugged onto both of them again, grateful that they were safe.

Then Annie looked into my face, "Are you hurt bad?"

I shook my head, "Not now honey. I couldn't feel better."

As Johnson dressed Penny, I took Jesse by the hand and said, "son there is someone here you have got to meet." We walked over to Andy and I said, "Andy this is my son Jesse. Jesse meet the mysterious Andy."

The boys grinned as Jesse said, "Wow, I am so glad to finally meet you."

Andy chuckled, "and I to meet you."

Jesse was so excited as he said, "Penny has talked so much about you that I feel I know you already."

Andy continued to smile as he said, "I hope we will continue to know each other."

"I'd like that," Jesse replied.

Penny clung to her father and kept saying that she was sorry and crying.

Johnson held her tight and kept reassuring her that she hadn't done anything to be sorry for.

Andy and Jesse looked at each other in a knowing way and started clowning around and soon had worked Penny and Johnson outside away from Grants body and had Penny laughing within minutes.

All of the excitement of the last couple of weeks had suddenly hit me and I was drained and a bit light headed so I walked over to the couch and sat down.

Becky and Annie came over and sat on either side of me. Becky asked, "are you sure that you're alright, Ricky. You look a little pale."

By this time I was shivering and Annie grabbed the blanket off the arm of the couch and wrapped it around me. "Ya Mom, you don't look so good."

I replied, "I think it's just my body trying to deal with all that has happened. I be fine in a few minutes."

Ned went out to his cruiser and radioed in. When he returned he had a grim look on his face as he said, "Ricky."

I looked up to face Ned. I had settled down some by this point and was feeling much better. Then I noticed the look on his face. "What's wrong Ned."

He shook his head in disbelief and said, "I just got off the horn with the U.S. Marshal's office and I can't believe that I have to do this, but . . ." He pulled out his cuffs and continued, Ricky Rogers, you're under arrest for kidnapping and the murder of Marshal Lee Grant. I'm afraid I'm going to have to ask you to stand up, turn around and put your hands behind your back."

I did what I was told and Ned put the cuffs on me and led me out to the cruiser. Everybody in the cabin started to protest as they followed us out the door. Jesse, Andy Johnson and Penny were still outside, but had heard the ruckus and joined in.

I turned and said, "No, stop," and they all froze in their tracks. "You're all safe now and I have no regrets. Besides, this will all be cleared up soon." I looked at my kids and said, "Take care of each other."

They nodded their head in disbelief.

Then I looked at Johnson, Andy and Penny. "Penny always remember somebody believed you and always did and you two take good care of her and be patient." They agreed. I turned to Becky. "You're the best. Keep the coffee hot."

"Always hot, waiting for you." She grinned but there were tears in her eyes too."

Ned looked at us all and said, "We should have this cleared up in no time, once we get a chance to tell the facts."

Becky asked, "How can this be happening Ned? We all know the truth here."

Ned shook his head, "It seems that Grant filed kidnapping charges already and a report saying that Ricky was after him, so with Ricky pulling the trigger, it looks like premeditated murder to the Marshal's Office."

"Didn't you tell them what happened," Jesse insisted.

I tried, Jesse, but it seems that slimeball had them all fooled."

Ned put me into the back of the cruiser and Johnson leaned down and said to me, "We're all behind you Ricky and we'll all be there to clear you and walk out the door proudly behind you when you're freed."

Wilder walked over to Johnson and stated, "Once I file my report she should be cleared of all charges."

I thanked him, as Ned and I drove away.

Wilder was right. It took some time, but I was cleared and settled into my quiet life in Westfield once more. I was a little older and a little wiser. I also knew that none of us would ever be quite the same as we were.